El Dorado County Library

Given in memory of
Mary Albanese
Teacher, Loving Grandmother &
Friend
Presented by
Dale Riehart & Susan
Baranowski

EL DORADO COUNTY LIBRARY
345 FAIR LANE
PLACERVILLE, CA 95667

The Last Girls of
POMPEII

~

The Last Girls of
POMPEII

KATHRYN LASKY

Viking

EL DORADO COUNTY LIBRARY
345 FAIR LANE
PLACERVILLE, CA 95667

Viking

Published by Penguin Group

Penguin Young Readers Group, 345 Hudson Street, New York, New York 10014, U.S.A.

Penguin Group (Canada), 90 Eglinton Avenue East, Suite 700, Toronto, Ontario,
Canada M4P 2Y3 (a division of Pearson Penguin Canada Inc.)

Penguin Books Ltd, 80 Strand, London WC2R 0RL, England

Penguin Ireland, 25 St Stephen's Green, Dublin 2, Ireland (a division of Penguin Books Ltd)

Penguin Group (Australia), 250 Camberwell Road, Camberwell, Victoria 3124,
Australia (a division of Pearson Australia Group Pty Ltd)

Penguin Books India Pvt Ltd, 11 Community Centre, Panchsheel Park,
New Delhi – 110 017, India

Penguin Group (NZ), 67 Apollo Drive, Mairangi Bay, Auckland 1311,
New Zealand (a division of Pearson New Zealand Ltd)

Penguin Books (South Africa) (Pty) Ltd, 24 Sturdee Avenue, Rosebank,
Johannesburg 2196, South Africa

Penguin Books Ltd, Registered Offices: 80 Strand, London WC2R 0RL, England

First published in 2007 by Viking, a division of Penguin Young Readers Group

1 3 5 7 9 10 8 6 4 2

Copyright © Kathryn Lasky, 2007
All rights reserved

LIBRARY OF CONGRESS CATALOGING-IN-PUBLICATION DATA
Lasky, Kathryn.
The last girls of Pompeii / by Kathryn Lasky.
p. cm.
Summary: Twelve-year-old Julia knows that her physical deformity will keep her from a
normal life, but counts on the continuing friend-ship of her life-long slave, Sura, until they
learn that both of their futures in first-century Pompeii are about to change for the worse.
ISBN-13: 978-0-670-06196-9 (hardcover)
[1. Family life—Rome—Fiction. 2. People with disabilities—Fiction. 3. Slavery—Fiction.
4. Pompeii (Extinct city)—Fiction. 5. Vesuvius (Italy)—Eruption, 79—Fiction.
6. Italy—Antiquities—Fiction.] I. Title.
PZ7.L327Las 2007   [Fic]—dc22   2006026663

Printed in U.S.A.
Set in Granjon
Book design by Nancy Brennan

EL DORADO COUNTY LIBRARY

The Last Girls of

POMPEII

~

One

IT WAS TOO EARLY FOR THE BIRDS.
So why had she awakened? Except for the
soft, rhythmic breathing of her slave, Sura,
sleeping at the foot of her bed, everything
was quiet. Silence lay over the villa as thickly as the August
heat. Nothing was stirring. But Julia was sure something
had. Had she heard some tiny noise? Or perhaps she had
felt something. Her eyes, now accustomed to the darkness
of the room, fell on the water glass beside her bed. That was
it! An infinitesimally small rattling sound. And yes, the surface of the water in the glass was trembling ever so slightly.
She watched it closely for several seconds. What made it do
this? Why, in the middle of the night, would water begin
to shiver? Throughout this long and torturously hot summer, there had been unexplained tremors—slight ones that
came up through the tiles of the floor or the paving stones
of the street. Her mother claimed that the gods were angry.

No, not the gods, just one in particular, Venus, the deity of the household of Cornelius Petreius and of the entire city.

Quietly Julia slipped her feet to the floor and walked across the tile, which felt cool compared to the air. She did not want to wake Sura. She opened one shutter just a bit and peered down into the garden. The slender columns surrounding it were bathed in moonlight. To Julia they looked like spirits, fragile and feminine like the young virgin priestesses who guarded the shrine of the vestals. There was a long rectangular pool filled by the water that flowed from the Venus fountain at the head of the garden. One of Rome's finest sculptors had made it for her mother and father when they were first married and moved into the villa. The figure was that of the goddess reclining on a large shell that overflowed gently with water. Her mother had insisted that the sound of water must be quiet. "Water must slip and not spout," Herminia Petreia had pronounced.

"What are you looking at?" a voice from behind Julia asked.

It was her slave, Sura. Julia instinctively used her right hand to grab her left arm, which was much smaller and hung limply at her side. This was just a startled reaction, not embarrassment. Sura had known her since birth. If anyone was accustomed to seeing the withered arm, it was Sura.

"Sura. I thought I was so quiet. I didn't mean to disturb you."

"It is too hot to sleep, mistress."

"I know." Then Julia nodded her head toward the pool. "Look how the reflection of the moon in the water trembles on this windless night."

"Hmm," was all that Sura said as she leaned forward to look. Her straight black hair swung like a curtain over one eye. So long and so straight. Julia envied her hair. She knew it was ridiculous to envy a slave, but she did nonetheless. Sura, at almost sixteen, was four years older than Julia. She was very pretty, and her eyes, like those of so many people from Thrace, were a soft green with flecks of gold.

Julia's hair was curly and uncontrollable. Her best feature were her dark eyes, which at first glance seemed almost black but were actually the deep blue of a night sky. Her worst feature, of course, was her left arm. Nearly as small as a baby's, it had never grown properly. But even though it was weak with barely any muscle, Julia had learned to do everything any girl her age could do with two arms. She could write and draw and even pluck the strings of a lyre. If it was just a question of usefulness, the arm wouldn't matter. But it wasn't as simple as that. The arm was not just different. It was ugly, and people stared at it. One hundred years ago, in the time of the Republic, she knew a deformity like hers had been referred to as the Curse of Venus. Julia was never exactly sure why a goddess of beauty would do such a thing, curse a family that worshipped her. She was grateful that her parents had never used this term in front of her. It was awful to be thought of as a cursed creature; it made her feel slightly less than human. Although it was hard to have been born flawed into a family that worshipped the goddess of beauty, Julia had wondered countless times what would have happened if she had been born during the harsher times of the Republic or to another family, one not so accepting of a deformity.

Once when she was very young, she had wondered aloud about this, and her older sister Cornelia had replied in the voice of great authority that she seemed to have been born with. "You would have been put out on a hillside to die. Simple as that!" Unfortunately for Cornelia, their mother had overheard. In a flash she had raced into the garden and delivered a solid slap to Cornelia, before folding Julia into her arms and nearly smothering her with kisses. Julia remembered Cornelia's stunned face. Julia was stunned, too. It was the only time Herminia had ever slapped one of her daughters.

But Julia knew that there was a great deal of truth in what Cornelia had said. Although times had changed, even now people tended to think of those born with deformities as something separate and apart. Not marriageable, for the gods would forbid that such flaws should be perpetuated. Ironically, however, once a deformed creature was brought into the world, people often believed that its defects gave special powers, sometimes frightening ones—especially if the deformed child was female. This belief was one reason why so many such infant girls were abandoned and left to die. Those who survived often became either priestesses or seers who with their powers could glimpse the future, interpret the past, and decipher the many hidden messages, signs, and omens that wove through the daily lives of ordinary people.

"It's true, Mother, you know it," Cornelia had protested, touching the red mark on her face. "She would have been left to die."

Herminia glared at her oldest daughter and nervously fingered the amber pendant of Cupid that hung around her neck. This was a habit she had when she grew agitated, as if she were invoking this god of love, the son of Venus, to come to her, be it to handle an unruly child or a stubborn husband. "If you don't want me to beat you like a slave, Cornelia, you shall never say such a thing again."

From her mother's arms, Julia had peeked triumphantly at Cornelia. Seeing Cornelia slapped was almost worth being born with a withered arm, she thought briefly. Almost, but not really.

Sura now touched her mistress's shoulder. "You must get to bed. Your mother plans to leave early tomorrow."

"Oh, no! The augurs again! Really?" Julia sighed. "Sura, my mother has had enough chickens slaughtered to feed everyone in Pompeii. All because of this stupid wedding date."

"And they all say the same thing," Sura sighed. "That Cornelia shouldn't get married on the twenty-fourth of August."

"Of course, it's Mundus Patet," said Julia. That was the day that the doors to the underworld were thought to open.

"But Cornelia says that's old fashioned," said Sura.

"Why doesn't Mother just say to Cornelia, 'Old fashioned or not, you're not getting married on that day'?"

Sura rolled her eyes. "Just say no to Cornelia? Tell her no wedding on that date? To delay? If they were to delay, the wedding couldn't be held until late September. Your father is going to visit the lumber merchants on August twenty-fifth and is away through most of September. There is no way Cornelia is waiting that long. And earlier is out of the question because of the Vulcanalia Festival on the twenty-third. No one ever gets married on a major festival. As it is, the twenty-fourth day of August is barely a month after Flavia's wedding. The weavers were very clear that they could not finish the wedding cloth any earlier. They had hardly removed the linen for Flavia's tunica recta from the loom. So earlier is out of the question, and later is too late for Cornelia's taste."

"Yes, I guess you're right, saying no to Cornelia is never easy."

Julia knew it was easier for her mother to keep dragging around to one more augur, one more priest, one more seer, than to say no to Cornelia. Cornelia could not abide the fact that her younger sister Flavia had been married before she was, even if it had only been a month ago. Julia herself felt that she had heard enough about weddings during this incredibly hot summer to last her a lifetime. Not only was wedding talk boring but weddings were as well. Too many strangers in the villa, business friends of her father's, and since last winter when her father had been elected a magistrate, there were even more people that had to be invited.

"You'd better go to bed now so you will be fresh for morning."

"I have an idea!" Julia said suddenly, her dark eyes gleaming. "Let's go swimming."

"Now?"

"Yes, now. We'll be very quiet. No splashes. It's so hot. Please? Remember we did it last summer? And this summer is much, much hotter than last summer."

Sura cocked her head as if she was thinking about it. "Well, all right, but if we get caught, you know who gets punished for being in the pool."

"I'll take the blame, I promise."

Sura laughed. "You always say that, Julia, and you know it's impossible. Slaves are here to take the blame. That is the way this world works. You might as well try to stop the sun from rising and setting, or the . . ." Sura searched for another example. ". . . or the tides from rising and falling."

"Well, it won't be that way when I grow up. Then I'll

give you your cap." Julia touched Sura's hair and tried to imagine what she would look like in one of the red freedom caps that freed slaves wore.

"But then, mistress Julia, who will take care of you, comb the snarls from your hair, rub your arm when it gets sore, take you to all the places in the city that your mother never would? Who will do that?"

"Well, you will. You see, when I'm grown up, I shall ask for all the money Mother and Father didn't spend on a dowry for me and then I'll set you free and pay you with that." Julia giggled. She knew it sounded silly, but it wasn't. Someday she would have a house of her own. She might even have a business of her own. It was not unheard of. Her mother had a friend, Claudia Plautia, who had never married and had inherited her father's wine brokerage business. There were no sons in Cornelius Petreius's family to inherit, just as there had been none in the family of Claudia Plautia. Herminia used to visit Claudia all the time, but now for some reason not as frequently. But right now Julia was too hot to think that far into the future.

"Let's go swimming," she said. "And if we keep our nightclothes on, they will be all wet and keep us cool as we sleep."

"Maybe," Sura said doubtfully. "But you must promise me you'll go to bed right away after we swim."

"I will. I promise."

The two girls padded softly along the loggia that led to

the stairs. Then, still walking softly, they passed through the summer dining room into the large garden. Statues were scattered throughout, and the white roses of which her mother was so proud glowed like ruffled moons on their trellises. Apricot trees lined the north wall, and the small orange fruits nestled in the darkness of the night. Julia went over to a tree and with a quick twist of her wrist plucked one and then a second.

"Here," she said, handing an apricot to Sura. They bit into the sweet flesh.

"Don't leave the pit in the pool," Sura said as Julia put her foot on the first shallow pool step. "Give it to me. I'll put it in this urn." An elaborately carved urn spilling with small white flowers stood at the top of the steps that descended into the pool.

The water was barely cool, but it still felt good. Julia loved the feeling of her tunic floating out from her. She loosened her long curly hair and lay back in the water. The locket around her neck bobbled. She touched it lightly. It was a special amulet called a bulla, a symbol of childhood worn by both boys and girls to ward off evil luck. Boys continued to wear theirs until they became men at about age fifteen. But every girl wore hers until she married. Julia's bulla, like that of her sisters, contained "the lock of Venus," a curl clipped from her mother's head on the day of Julia's birth and tucked into the bronze locket. She wondered what her mother had thought on the day of Julia's birth when she saw the withered arm and put the bulla on its chain around her neck. Did she think any worse luck could befall her child than already had? Since the worst in one sense had already happened to Julia, what could the bulla protect her from?

Sura swam up beside her. "Feels nice, doesn't it?"

"Wonderful," Julia said. "I wish I could invent a bed that could be used in the water. Just think of it, Sura, how nice it would feel to sleep in this pool all night." She giggled at the thought.

"Shhhh," Sura cautioned her.

Julia put her feet on the bottom of the pool. She looked down at the tunic that radiated around her. "Look! Aren't I just like a flower with petals now?"

On the water's surface, stars floated in great drifts, and through the branches of the trees overhead chips of moonlight like white moths fluttered in the night. Pushing off with her feet, Julia very quietly began swimming toward the reclining Venus on her half shell. She stopped just under the lip of the shell and put her head back, letting the water from the fountain pour over her face. *Am I an offense to you, Venus, goddess of our family? Were you punishing my mother when I was born? Why?*

Though she would never admit it to her parents, Julia, of all her family members, was the most skeptical of the gods and all the superstitions surrounding their religion. She believed like her favorite cousin Marcus, who was fourteen, that there could be other laws at work. As Marcus had said to her one day, "It's all nonsense. These augurs make stupid pronouncements like if lightning strikes a temple it's a sign from the gods. But there is metal on the roof of the temple of Jupiter and not on the temple of Apollo, which is practically next door. So couldn't that make a difference?"

Julia had thought about what he said. Marcus was smart, very smart. He had read most of the books of Pliny the Elder, the great scholar who wrote about almost everything one could think of.

"There's probably some simple explanation for why your arm is that way," Marcus had said.

"Like what?" Julia had asked.

"Well, maybe you were upside down or something for a while in your mother's womb."

Julia didn't know if there was a simple explanation, but she certainly did not think it was as simple as a punishment from Venus.

Now she hoisted herself onto the shell and looked at the figure of Venus. The sculptor had taken the most time with the goddess's body. He had rushed the face, and it seemed rather blank to Julia. She touched the stone chin. *It's just stone,* she thought. *Stone and some artist's dream of a beautiful woman.* Julia had a sudden thought. If indeed there were a goddess Venus, with passions and feelings, capable of jealousy and love, might she not be angry that this artist had rushed the sculpting of her face, leaving her to look dull and slightly stupid? And if so, wouldn't she take vengeance on the artist, not on the client's family? A very interesting question. She must remember to discuss it with Marcus. He would be coming for dinner the next evening.

Even in a short time out of the water she had grown hot. So she slipped back in and resumed floating on her back. Sura drifted next to her and studied the stars overhead. She often wondered about the stars. Did the same stars drift over Thrace? She could barely remember the time when she and her brother had been captured and sold into slavery. The memories of her mother and father were so dim. Their village, the farm—she remembered a bed that she had shared with her grandmother. But she didn't really remember her grandmother. However, she must have loved them all, her parents and grandmother. She had tried to get her older brother, Bryzos, who was captured with her and trained as a gladiator, to tell her stories. But he didn't like to. It made him sad, he said. *I can't even be sad*, Sura thought, *because I can't remember enough to be sad*. And that, she knew, in its own odd way, was the saddest thing of all. And yet she felt nothing. It was hard to miss something if you couldn't remember it. Julia floated closer to Sura, and their hands touched in the water.

What Sura would truly miss, if they were ever separated, would be Julia. Julia and her family had marked the beginning of Sura's life. Her earliest real memories went back to the time of Julia's birth. She remembered everyone crying because the baby had been born with an ugly arm. But to Sura she was perfect. And taking care of Julia made her feel important. Even though she was barely five years old at the time of Julia's birth, Sura and the wet nurse were the only ones who could quell the baby's crying. And when Julia was weaned, she and Sura grew even closer. Sura looked over at her now.

"This is fun," Julia said. "I love doing things when everyone else is asleep. It's like a spice. It adds flavor to whatever you're doing." Sura chuckled softly. Julia had such an original way of saying things.

"But it's time to go in. You have an early day tomorrow," Sura said.

"Just one more minute."

"You promised, Julia!" Sura said, trying not to raise her voice.

"All right." Julia swam toward the stairs. "I still don't see why I have to go along to yet another augur."

"Your mother wants you there."

"Papa doesn't go."

"He can't. He has his shipping business to run, and now that he's a magistrate, he has to go to the forum. Come on to bed. I will fan you," Sura urged.

"I don't think Mother likes it that he is a magistrate."

"Now why would that be? It's a great honor."

"You have to spend money when you're a magistrate—

putting on games and such for the people. That means less money for weddings and for repairs to the Temple of Venus."

Sura looked at her closely, pressing her lips together and making a low "hmm" sound as she considered what Julia had just said.

"Believe me, it's true, Sura. I know about these things. It's politics."

"I suppose you're right," Sura replied.

Julia slipped into her bed wet, not bothering to pull up the thin sheet. Sura crouched by the wall and pulled a string that was attached to a date-palm frond and began to fan her. The drafts from the fan, although they were warm, were better than nothing. Julia thought that in all this heat it was impossible to even imagine that a cool current of air could be stirred up. The air had hardly moved for days, for weeks. There was not even a ripple on the surface of the bay, which lay less than a thousand feet from their villa. The blue water looked as if it had been enameled.

I might as well be enameled myself, Julia thought. *Nothing moves, nothing stirs, nothing breathes. It's as if everything has been holding its breath all summer. I want it to be autumn. Cornelia will certainly be married by then. Flavia is already married. I will be the only child left at home. That will be nice.*

There was a sudden pocket of silence in the night, and Julia was jerked back from the brink of sleep. The soft whisks of the palm frond had ceased, its cooling breeze swallowed in the nighttime heat. Sura must have fallen asleep. Odd, Julia thought, how something stopping, the absence of sound, could awaken you. She yawned and turned over, pushing her dead arm out from under her so it would not be numb in the morning. *Numb, enameled, still, dead.* So many words to describe feelings that were not really feelings at all but the absence of them.

Two

 JULIA FELT HER SHOULDER BEING shaken. "Get up, get up, mistress." Sura was bending over her, the long black hair brushing her cheek. "Your mother wants to set off within the hour."

"You know that means two hours, Sura. She's always late."

"Get up now, please."

"Can you tell her I have a stomachache and it will only get worse when I see those augurs slitting chickens and pulling out their guts!" She made a phlegmy sound of disgust in the back of her throat.

"You tried that last time, Julia. It didn't work."

"All right, all right! I just don't see why I have to go. There's no reason."

"You're mother wants it—that's reason enough. It's customary."

A few minutes later, after Sura had helped her put on her tunic, Julia sat in front of the mirror as Sura dressed her hair.

"Up or down?" Sura asked.

"Up—all the way up. It's too hot to have it hanging around my shoulders. When is my fringe going to be long enough to pull back?"

"Not yet, mistress."

"Can you slick it back with some water and pomade?"

"I'll try."

Julia observed her reflection in the mirror. She looked so different from her sisters in every respect, not just her arm. Her eyes were the darkest blue, while theirs were bright cornflower blue like their mother's. Her hair was not black but a rather boring brown, while theirs was blonde, also like their mother. But Julia's mother did help her own hair color along with a dye made of animal fat and ash. And Julia was the only one with freckles that no amount of powder seemed to cover, especially in the summer, when they stretched across her nose and cheeks. Julia didn't really think they were ugly, but they violated all conventional standards of beauty.

Julia could now hear her mother's voice drifting out through the shutters of her dressing room next door, as the ornatrix who came each morning to style her hair worked. It was a soft argument between her mother and father. They had been having this squabble all summer. Julia could only catch fragments, but it did not take too much imagination to fill in the rest. She could almost see her mother fingering the amber Cupid pendant.

"Now, five thousand sesterces, it's not that much, Cornelius."

"It's half a wedding," her father replied.

"But not nearly as much as the games you're putting on," her mother countered.

"Herminia, we have been through this before. I am a magistrate now, newly elected to the ordo."

"The ordo, the ordo, that's all I ever hear about. . . ." Her mother's despairing voice dwindled away to a low whisper, but Julia knew they were talking about her father's election as one of the magistrates who headed the city council, the ordo. Her father's position in Pompeii in the past three or four years had steadily risen. He was no longer simply a wealthy shipbuilder. Now he was a distinguished leader of the city. It was expected that leaders would sponsor gladiatorial games for the entertainment of the public, and the games were very expensive.

"And Pansa," Julia heard her father say.

He was speaking of Cuspius Pansa, to whom they were now related by Flavia's marriage to his son.

"We should be proud . . ." He paused. "We *are* proud to be related to the family that has contributed more to the restoration of the amphitheater than any other family in Pompeii. There had not been games in this city for several

years. And now look what Cuspius Pansa has done in just
the last three years. We have games again!" Seventeen years
before, there had been a devastating earthquake that had
left the amphitheater in ruins. "Herminia, it is expected
that I should involve myself in civic philanthropy, and we
are now related through marriage to the family of all families that is the most responsible for the rebuilding of the
amphitheater and sponsorship of games. This is an obliga-
tion expected of me both as a magistrate and because of the
connection between our families."

"I know, Cornelius. But it was not only the amphithea-
ter that was damaged in the earthquake. The Temple of
Venus was as well. We could become to the temple what
Cuspius Pansa is to the games and the amphitheater."

"But two weddings in one summer. We cannot be all
things at the same time, Herminia." Then he muttered
something about goddesses and daughters, but Julia could
not hear it clearly. She really didn't need to hear it all. The
gist of her parents' heated discussion was all too familiar to
her: the temple versus the amphitheater. Her mother could
not understand how an arena for bloody games could be
restored prior to what she called "an arena for a goddess,"
and not just any goddess—Venus Pompeiana, the protect-
ing goddess of the city. What galled her even more was that
the temples of other gods, lesser ones in her opinion, had
already been restored. In particular she objected to the restoration of the Temple of Isis, the most completely rebuilt of

any of the temples through the extreme generosity of Numerius Popidius Ampliatus—formerly a slave!

Julia rolled her eyes at Sura. "See, I told you Mother would be late. They have to have their daily argument. Has Father already seen his clients?"

"Most of them. You just be waiting for your mother in the lararium for morning worship when they come down. Promise me."

"All right." Julia sighed as she stood up and slipped her deep rose–colored palla over her shoulder, hiding her arm.

By the time Julia descended to the main floor of the villa, she could hear the impatient hubbub of the remainder of her father's "clients" as they were called, awaiting their patron's arrival. A wealthy Roman citizen was obliged, if not by law than by custom, to distribute money, food, or small gifts daily to those upon whom he was dependent for votes and small services, and to his freed slaves. In return the patron received the support of the clients in his own endeavors, which might range from campaigning for an office in the civic government to tracking down a runaway slave to finding a good rate for an expensive wine for a celebration.

As Julia entered the lararium, she saw her older sister Cornelia already kneeling in front of the shrine. The death masks of her great-grandparents and her grandfather hung to one side of a tall cupboard. Cornelia looked up as if to say, *You're late again.* In her hands she held the petals of one of the white roses from the garden as her morning offering to their household gods. Julia had brought a gold cup of scented water to set on the altar. She kneeled next to Cornelia and whispered, "Don't look at me that way. I'm not late. Mother's not even here yet."

"I wasn't looking at you any way," Cornelia replied coldly.

"Yes, you were," Julia argued.

Herminia Petreia bustled in with her husband.

"Girls, girls! Quit this squabbling," Herminia scolded.

Why don't they quit theirs? Julia mused.

"Mother," Cornelia whined. "She is so childish."

"Me, childish!" Julia exclaimed. "What about you? You're about to be married. You're eighteen. I'm twelve."

"Stop it, both of you!" Their mother said firmly.

Behind Herminia and her husband Cornelius, the rest of the household slaves filed into the lararium. Cornelius, as the head of the family, also functioned as the priest in this morning worship. He began with his usual invocation bending before the masks of his parents and those of his wife to thank them for their wisdom and goodness. As he concluded, Herminia stepped forward holding a plate with a small pile of crumbs. It was believed that the lares, or the spirits of the family's ancestors, resided in the floor. The crumbs that had fallen during the course of the previous day's meals were swept up, and an offering was made to them. Herminia kneeled and presented the plate of crumbs.

As soon as she had risen, Cornelius opened the cupboard to reveal the representations of Venus and the other household gods. The cupboard was made of wood and looked quite ordinary on the outside, but when opened it revealed a splendid interior that had been painted to look like marble. Within the cupboard was a miniature temple, the Temple of Venus as it had appeared before the earthquake. This was Julia's favorite part of the ceremony. There were "marble" steps leading up to a portico supported by gleaming "marble" columns, and perfectly centered was a tiny real marble statue of Venus with her golden girdle. Flanking the temple on each side was a niche. The one to the left revealed a painting of Jupiter, the father of the gods. The one on the right held a painted image of Juno, wife of Jupiter, and next to Juno in the same niche was Minerva, goddess of wisdom. These three represented the Capitoline Triad. After the doors were opened, there was another short prayer, the Calling, a greeting and giving of thanks to these gods. When it concluded, Cornelia offered her rose petals to the triad. Following Cornelia, Julia came with her golden bowl of scented water from which she sprinkled a few drops in front of each of the gods and goddesses.

This was followed by long, and for Julia unendurable, moments of silent worship, in which she tried to guess what each of her family members was praying for. Very little effort was necessary these days. She knew all too well their prayers. Her mother was hoping for at least two augurs to agree to a wedding date for Cornelia. She also wanted a windfall of money so that she could put on a wedding worthy of their social position and repair the architrave, the recessed panel with the beautiful sculpture that adorned the main facade of the Temple of Venus. Cornelia was praying that her mother would not insist on two augurs but just settle for one. Their father was praying that somehow he could come up with an extra ten thousand sesterces for the restoration of the temple his wife so dearly wanted. And Julia was just praying for autumn to come, when the wedding would be over and the weather cooler, and her tutor would return from Rome. Then they could begin lessons again and forget all about weddings!

Three

A FEATHER DRIFTED LAZILY OVER the bloody tangle of chicken guts that lay on the slab of marble. A haruspex, an augur who specialized in interpreting animal entrails, crouched over to study them. His toga was spattered with spurts of blood. Julia couldn't help but wonder how many togas he went through in one day. The heat rose in waves, rippling the air. Everything appeared swimmy, and the entrails themselves behind this pulsing scrim of air seemed to move ever so slightly. Did Julia feel a small tremor beneath her feet? She saw the flash of the haruspex's eyes as they slid nervously to look beyond the marble slab at the distant hills. *He felt it, too!* This certainly could not be a good sign if at the very moment the entrails were read the earth trembled. Julia stole a glance at her mother and Cornelia. They were so intent on the haruspex that Julia doubted they had even felt it. Jupiter! how many of these

idiots did they have to go to? Yesterday it had been an augur who specialized in thunderbolts, because two nights before there had been dry lightning over Mount Vesuvius. He didn't precisely say no to the date, but nor did he give an true affirmation. So off they went to see the haruspex Lucretius, who although just a beginner was considered quite good.

"Possibly, possibly," the augur was now saying. "You say the twenty-fourth day of August is what you have planned on for the marriage of Cornelia to Cassius Marcellus? Fine young man, fine young man. And what sign was he born under?" All while he spoke, he pored over the steaming entrails. Julia could feel the mounting excitement of her mother and sister. Cornelia's mouth was half open as if she were holding her breath in anticipation. The color rose in their mother's cheeks.

Is this fellow an idiot? Julia thought. *The ground just shook!* She had felt it, and she knew that the haruspex had as well. Marcus was right. These fools said whatever was necessary to get a good fee. But would her mother sink to bribery? Maybe it wasn't so much that her mother had bribed him outright. Perhaps he had just read her like a book, read her urgency, her hopes, as well as her denial. This man was probably better at reading human minds than chicken guts. And now he was actually saying what they had so longed to hear. "I would see no problem with the date of the twenty-fourth day of this month. None whatsoever." Cornelia let out a little squeal of delight. Their mother smiled broadly.

And from a pouch she carried under her palla she slipped Lucretius some gold coins.

As they were about to walk back to the litter that awaited them, Julia's palla slipped off her shoulder, revealing her withered arm. Her mother and sister were ahead and did not hear the haruspex gasp. But when she turned to look at the him, she saw that his eyes were glazed with fear. What was wrong with him? She gave him a scowling look. And then it dawned on her. *I wonder if he thinks I have more powers than he does.*

By the time Julia climbed into the litter, her mother and Cornelia were already arguing. "But Mother, why do we have to go there?"

"I want just one more opinion, that's all."

"But what if she says no?"

"I think we can still go ahead, dear. I would just feel better if she would say yes, too."

"Are we going to the Sibyl of Sarnus?" Julia groaned.

Both she and Cornelia hated going to this sibyl, who lived in a cave at the mouth of the Sarnus River near the harbor of Pompeii. They were always left to wait well outside of the cave, but Julia hated seeing her mother go into it to meet with the sibyl. This particular sybil was said to read the eyes of fish, which both Julia and her sister both found horribly disgusting even though they didn't have to witness it.

To reach the Sibyl of Sarnus they had to pass by their

own villa again. There the slaves who were carrying them were exchanged for fresh litter bearers, due to the extreme heat. This did not take long, and they were soon on their way again. As they approached the sacred precincts of the Temple of Venus, Julia saw Cornelia touch her bulla. She knew what her sister was praying for—that the Sibyl of Sarnus would not spoil things. Her mother was most likely thinking what ten thousand sesterces could do to rebuild the wrecked sanctuary of her goddess.

They passed through the Gate of Forensa, and soon enough they were in a narrow street in the midst of the port. The harbor was crammed with double-ended two-masted trading ships, many built in the shipyard of Julia's father. This passage through the port was almost worth the trip to the Sibyl of Sarnus. There was everything from anywhere that anyone could imagine. Julia looked out from the curtained window of the litter to see if the brilliantly colored parrot that had been for sale the week before had been sold.

"Is the parrot still there, Julia?" Cornelia asked suddenly.

"No, I think he's been sold." The cage swung now with a new parrot.

"Oh dear, that one's not nearly so pretty. Papa should have bought that one for you!"

Julia turned and looked at her sister. Cornelia could be so nice sometimes, especially when she wasn't thinking about weddings and being the unmarried eldest daughter. But something in her had hardened after the humiliation of her broken first engagement to Gaius Horatius Fortunatus, who had run off with a slave girl. She wished that old Cornelia would return—the one who thought about parrots that caught her sister's eye, or who had rescued a dormouse once from the cook's cleaver just because Julia had taken a fancy to it. Stolen it right out from under cook's nose, she had!

They passed by the horse trader and his slave, a Nubian as black as charred wood but with sea-blue eyes. The slave stood holding an old nag that a prospective buyer was haggling over with the trader, who did not look as if he would lower his price. The scent of spices from India suddenly cut through the ripe port smell. Julia pulled the curtain aside to get a better sniff. As she leaned out the window of the litter, she caught sight of a monkey turning somersaults to the delight of several small urchins.

Julia's eyes feasted on the scene, while her mother and sister pressed perfumed handkerchiefs to their noses. But Julia didn't mind the smell, which was a heady mixture of animal dung, baitfish, exotic spices, human sweat, and salt air. It was all over too quickly, and soon they were on the Stabiae road that led to the Sarnus. Julia sank back in her cushioned seat as the slaves jogged on with the litter. Their mother had dozed off, and Cornelia gazed out the window, unseeing of anything but her own dreams.

Julia spotted the three large rocks rising out of the sea. The water became less blue as the silt of the river swirled out into the bay. They were very near now. She sank back against the cushions. The most she could hope for at this point was that her mother would not spend too long with the sibyl and the sibyl would not come to the mouth of the cave. Julia imagined a gruesome apparition of a woman twined with garlands of fishes' eyeballs. *Fish eyeballs—what could be worse?* she thought. Well, there was something. Snakes. Julia didn't like snakes. Yes, that would be worse.

Four

THE GROUND WAS DUSTY, AND the only shade available was a sparsely leafed poplar tree. Cornelia chose to remain in the litter, but Julia was just too hot. She went over to the poplar and sat on a rock beneath it. If a leaf could look weary, these limp and shriveled ones with their pittance of shade did. The slightly sulfurous smell that emanated from the river's mouth seemed stronger today.

Julia saw a small fish jump. She wondered how long it had until the sibyl caught it for her prophesies. *Prophetic fish, ridiculous!* Were she and Marcus the only two people in the entire Roman Empire who thought it was completely irrational to think one could tell the future through the innards of animals, let alone a fish's eyeballs? Julia always had a terrible image of the sibyl pawing over these eyeballs, rolling them about in her palm, like dice about to be thrown. Or maybe she squished them to see what popped out. Julia couldn't wait to get home and plunge into the pool. Soon she heard the voices of her mother and the sibyl echoing from within the cave. The voices drew closer. She sighed. The sibyl was coming with her mother!

"Julia, Julia!" her mother called. "Come dear, the sibyl would like to see you."

"What about me?" Cornelia said, stepping from the litter.

Their mother appeared at the cave mouth. Behind her there was a shadowy figure. Julia hesitantly walked to the edge and Cornelia came up beside her. The glare of the midday sun was so fierce that they had to squint. The cave shadows looked cool, almost tempting. The sibyl stayed well within them. She never came out far enough for them to see her. For all the times they had visited, she had remained a shrouded, misty figure made of half-light and cave shadows. They had never even glimpsed her face—their mother always preferred to visit with her alone—but even so, Julia worried that some strange quirk of light and shadow might reveal her. And if one chose to live in a cave with only fish for company, well, Julia could only imagine someone very strange looking.

"Greetings," the sibyl said. It was the voice that always surprised Julia. One expected a sibyl to have the creaking voice of an old lady, but this one didn't. She did not sound any older than Julia's mother.

"Greetings," Cornelia and Julia both replied.

"Cornelia, your mother will discuss with you my thoughts on your marriage."

"Yes, thank you very much." The sibyl's name was unknown to Julia and Cornelia. Everyone simply called her the Sibyl of Sarnus, and unlike some seers or oracles, she did not like being called Holy One. Thus she went entirely nameless, which made her even more mysterious.

"Julia," said the Sibyl of Sarnus.

"Yes?"

"You are quite overheated, child, I can see." Cornelia shot Julia a look as if to say, *Why is the attention on you? I'm to be the bride.* "Well, take care, my dear, and remember as hot as it is now, when snow comes in summer, that is the time to leave."

Julia was confounded, and she could see from the expression on her mother's face that she was as well.

"Come, girls!" Julia's mother said. "We had better get home." But before leaving, Herminia turned, stepped back into the cave briefly, and leaned into the shadows. She whispered something to the sibyl, but the voices were swallowed by the void. Julia thought how strange this was. Did the cave have no echoes, or had her mother drawn her face so close to the sibyl's as she was whispering that no sound could escape? The notion of her mother pressing her mouth to the sibyl's ear was revolting.

The instant their mother climbed into the litter, Cornelia was peppering her with questions. "So what did she say, Mother? What did she say? Does she think it's all right? Did you tell her what the haruspex said?"

"No, of course I didn't tell her what Lucretius said. I didn't want to influence her by repeating other augurs' words."

"Well, what did she say?" Cornelia pressed.

Herminia Petreia inhaled deeply. "She said that it would be better for you not to marry on that day."

"No!" Cornelia protested, and tears immediately began spilling from her eyes, making slick tracks down her flushed cheeks.

Herminia took her daughter's hand. "Calm yourself, dear, and listen to me. She said if the marriage *must* take place on the twenty-fourth day of the month, then by all means marry early in that day. Begin the ceremonies in the morning with the auspex on hand." The auspex was an augur who would preside over the couple's offering of an animal sacrifice to the gods. "It just means," Herminia continued, "that we shall have to begin preparing you before dawn. I shall have your father cancel his audience with the clients. But you must remember that the day before is the festival of Vulcanalia. We cannot celebrate too long into the night if we must get up before dawn."

"Oh, Mother!" Cornelia's tears still stained her face, but

her eyes brimmed with joy. "I'll be up before anyone. I don't mind cutting the Vulcanalia short."

"Well, I do!" Julia muttered.

Cornelia ignored her and continued chatting away gaily. "I'll have Aria begin to fix my hair well before dawn."

"You shall do no such thing. A simple slave girl to do the wedding tutulus! You know how difficult it is to part the hair just so and then wind the sections on top of the head, and all the pinning and the false hair as well! No. Only an ornatrix can do that style."

"Yes, Mother," Cornelia replied meekly, but she could hardly conceal her happiness and her excitement.

"And Julia, the ornatrix will fix your hair as well!"

"Mine?" Julia was surprised. But she wasn't about to argue. When Flavia had been married, Sura and not an ornatrix had fixed Julia's hair. She couldn't imagine why it was different now.

The conversation continued. Julia was soon bored as her mother and Cornelia nattered on about hairstyles and false hair and how the veil should be attached. The words of the sibyl came back and kept weaving through her thoughts. What in the world did they mean, and why had she said them to Julia now? Snow in summer? That would be a blessing in her mind.

They were taking a different route back through the city and passed through the Stabian Gates. She heard her mother give a sniff of disgust as they went by the Temple of

Isis. Herminia considered both the patron, a former slave, and the Egyptian goddess herself unworthy. The worship of Isis, once popular with the lower classes, was spreading to the aristocracy. All of this added up in Herminia's mind to a grave offense toward the patron goddess of the city and their own family. "Look at the crowds at that temple!" she exclaimed.

"But, Mother," Cornelia said, "it's the time. It's half-past two."

"Oh, of course, I forgot."

Twice a day the worshipers at the Temple of Isis celebrated their goddess in a ceremony called the ritual of the lustral waters, in which the sacred water of the Nile, the river of the goddess's origins, was venerated.

"Imagine," Herminia continued, "a former slave restored that temple, and not only that—he installed his six-year-old son as priest!"

"Was Popidius Celsinus only six?" Julia exclaimed.

"Yes, and now he's a member of the ordo. You can buy your way into anything in this town!" Herminia huffed.

"Mother," Cornelia said suddenly, "for the wedding, could we have the doves like Valeria had, the ones with the rose-scented wings?"

Julia yawned and leaned her head back against the pillow.

Five

 JULIA WOKE UP AS THE LITTER WAS set down. She had drifted off into a thin nap as her mother and Cornelia had begun one of their ceaseless conversations about wedding details. The last thing Julia remembered was something about doves with rose-scented wings being released at Valeria Octavia's wedding.

"Home? Already?"

"No, dear, the baths," her mother replied.

"Mother!"

Julia hated going to the women's baths, which occupied an entire block near the Via Stabiana. Because of the deformity of her arm, it was sheer torture for Julia to get undressed in front of other women and girls. Usually her mother was sensitive to this and they bathed in the private baths of their home, but because of the extreme heat of the last several days her mother had directed that the bath fires not be lit, as they made the house too hot.

Since the earthquake seventeen years ago, only the women's section of the Stabian Baths had been rebuilt. Her father went to the Forum Baths closer to the house, but they had only a small women's section.

"We won't linger," Herminia said. "But I feel absolutely caked with grime."

Cornelia, of course, was terribly excited. The baths were a great place for gossip, and now she could announce her wedding date with complete confidence.

Julia pressed herself close to her mother as they entered the building, and followed a winding corridor to the changing room. A large lady with skin the color of cinnamon and one bright white tooth that protruded like a fang from her mouth handed them towels. Julia's mother slid six asses toward her, the price of admission. The Petreia women then proceeded through an arch into the changing room.

"Valeria!" Cornelia squealed, and ran across the tiled floor to where a naked girl was just placing her folded tunic in a niche above the red stone bench. "It's August twenty-fourth for certain."

"Wonderful! And the doves, are you doing the doves?"

"I don't know." Cornelia turned to her mother with beseeching eyes. "Mother, are we doing the doves?"

"Oh, you should, Herminia Petreia," Valeria said eagerly, and turned toward Herminia. She patted the small mound that rose on her stomach.

"Oh, my!" Herminia exclaimed. "I did not know. How far along are you?"

"Three months. And it's the doves. They say the doves insure fertility, you know."

Another woman snorted. "I am sure it was not just the doves, Valeria Octavia. Your dear Octavius had something to do with it. I've heard from my son, who sees him at the gymnasium, that he is quite well suited to the task."

There was a ripple of laughter through the changing room.

This was another thing that Julia hated about coming to the baths—the constant joking about everyone's private parts. It was one thing when she and Sura told bawdy jokes to one another. But they never did it in public. And Julia felt so left out here. It was unlikely that she would ever marry, or share a bed with a husband, or have a baby grow inside her.

She hurriedly undressed and then, hiding her arm beneath the towel, walked quickly to the other side of the changing room and stepped down into the cold pool. The chilly water felt wonderful as she sank down up to her shoulders and tipped her head back against the edge. The pillars of the room were painted with large boats with their sails unfurled. Julia imagined herself on one of those boats, sailing straight out across the bay to a distant horizon, away from weddings, away from chicken gut–reading augurs . . . just away on a boundless blue sea.

Within a short time she was thoroughly chilled. She climbed from the pool and took her towel.

"Leaving already, Julia?" Valeria asked.

"I'm cold."

"Skin and bones!" Cornelia added. "Not much to snuggle up to." She giggled and poked her own ample breasts from the water.

Julia tucked her chin down and walked rapidly to the next room, the tepidarium, where the water was warmer. No sooner had she slipped into the pool than her mother arrived. "I'm going to have a talk with Cornelia. This beastly behavior of hers must stop."

"It won't," Julia said glumly. "She enjoys it."

"Julia, you must realize that Cornelia is weak."

"Weak?"

"Well, not weak, exactly, but insecure. She'll never get over . . ." Herminia hesitated. "Well, you know that business with Gaius Horatius Fortunatus." The business Herminia was referring to was the broken engagement.

"But that was years ago." And besides, Julia thought as she had so often before, it wasn't weakness at all but quite the reverse. Something had hardened in her sister after that.

"It doesn't matter. And then when her younger sister was married before her, if only by weeks . . ." Herminia glanced over her shoulder. "Shush, here she comes."

Cornelia and Valeria had now been joined by two more of their friends. There were gales of giggles as the mosaics on the pool floor, which depicted both male and female nudes, gave rise to many more bawdy jokes. The girls became quite raucous as they began a game that involved stepping on the genitals of nude depictions of Mercury. Some older women in the pool frowned, and one called out to stop all the splashing. Herminia moved over to Cornelia and rapped her on the shoulder sharply.

"You are about to become a married woman! Behave!"

Cornelia, already flushed from the warmth of the baths, turned redder.

"Sorry, Mother."

Herminia was stepping out of the pool. Cornelia followed her and Julia to the last of the three baths, the hottest one, the caldarium. Of all the rooms, this one was the prettiest. The floor was covered with white mosaic tiles framed with a black strip. The walls were red and decorated with garlands and marsh landscapes showing water plants and geese. On the east side was a marble pool with hot water and on the opposite side one with cool water. Back and forth the bathers crossed the room, and then finally Herminia motioned to her daughters that it was time to go. But before they returned to the dressing room from the baths, they wrapped themselves in their large towels and strolled under the porticoes in the gardens, sipping drinks to restore lost fluids.

Returning to their litter, they felt refreshed and scrubbed of every grain of dirt.

"Hurry!" Herminia ordered the litter bearers. She drew closed the curtains. It was as if every second in the street was a threat of contamination to their newly scoured skin. They were, thought Julia, like flowers out of water, every petal at risk of turning brown at the edges.

Julia looked at her mother. She glowed a soft, peachy pink. Her eyes were like the blue mist of the Bay of Naples, and her long dark-blonde lashes cast a filigree of shadows across her fine cheekbones. Was there ever a more beautiful woman? *Venus blessed she is,* thought Julia. *Yes, blessed by the goddess of love and beauty.*

Six

 "MIGHT JULIA ACCOMPANY ME, mistress?" Sura asked after Herminia Petreia had given her the list of morning errands to perform, most of which related to the upcoming wedding.

Herminia pursed her lips as she contemplated the request. "Well, I suppose if you are to go to the fuller with all this linen you will need a litter. So Julia could go with you." She gestured toward the neatly stacked folded fabric, newly woven, from which Cornelia's wedding clothes would be made. "Just make sure she doesn't get overheated. And as long as Julia will be with you, you might as well go to the shop of Fabulla and see if she has any false locks to match her hair. Two will be sufficient."

"Yes, mistress."

"And don't dally, Sura. There is so much to be done and so little time before the wedding."

"Don't worry, mistress."

"Yes, I know I can count on you, Sura." Her eyes lingered on Sura's face. They clouded for just a moment. Sura swallowed nervously and wondered why there seemed to be this tinge of regret in Herminia Petreia's eyes. Mostly, however, Sura was flooded with relief that her mistress had agreed to let Julia come with her. She hated going to the fullery of Stephanus, where their clothes were laundered and newly woven fabric was finished and made pliable. In the past, the fuller had made unwanted advances toward Sura, but surely the swinish man would not try anything lewd in front of her master's daughter.

"We'll go to the fuller's first," Sura announced as she and Julia stepped into the litter. She wanted to get that part over with as soon as possible. Julia was prattling on about how sick she was of weddings, and how impossible Cornelia was. Sura had been hearing this for weeks on end, and she was also weary of the wedding talk but, she had to admit, just as tired of Julia's constant complaining. At the moment, however, Julia's complaints were not her concerns. It was the fuller. *What if he* does *try something in front of Julia?* His advances had become bolder. And she had heard rumors about him in the marketplace. She knew a woman who knew a woman who knew of another woman—not even a woman really, a mere girl—whom Stephanus had bought as a concubine. She was very young and very pretty, but he grew tired of her and sold her to a brothel. The girl had been pointed out to her just a few weeks before. Now she looked like an old woman, a hag. Sura might be a slave, but her life was just fine as far as she was concerned. She was a house slave of the highest kind. She never scrubbed floors. She ran important errands for her mistress. But most important, she was entrusted with the care of Julia.

"You say that we are to go to Fabulla's for hair locks for me?" Julia asked.

"Yes."

"I hate those coils. They remind me of snakes hanging over my ears."

"Well, don't worry. She probably won't be able to match your color." Sura laughed as she watched Julia unpin one of her braids from its neat coil and cross her eyes to examine its tail. "Now see, you've undone my artful work."

"Sorry. Just wanted to check, that's all. Not a very pretty color, is it?"

"It's a fine color, and it's yours. You watch. Cornelia's hair will be dry as straw if she keeps dying it the way she does."

"Mother's isn't, and she's been dying it longer than Cornelia."

"She has more natural oils."

"Can you pin my braid back for me?"

"Not while we're jiggling along. That's one of those sharp pins. You want to get stuck?"

"Not really." Julia tucked the pin in a fold of her tunic.

"Oh!" Sura let out a small startled gasp. "We're here so quickly."

At the corner of the fullery, they saw a man relieving himself into a large pot by the door. Urine was the single most important ingredient for the work of the fuller. Newly woven clothes or clothes needing to be cleaned were soaked in it for bleaching. The urine made them softer and easier to work with. Sura's heart sank as Stephanus, the owner of the fullery, came out to greet them. He looked boldly at Sura.

"You have brought me the daughter of a citizen! Another vote, perhaps, from your honorable father, Flavius Cornelius Petreius." He nodded at the inscription painted on the wall of his shop—SUPPORT THE ELECTION OF STEPHANUS AS DECURION. But the entire time Stephanus spoke, his eyes crawled over Sura, and he never even glanced at Julia.

"I have brought you cloth to be finished," Sura snapped.

"Well, step inside. Let's see how much you have. Your young mistress—the name is Julia?—she can wait outside." He did not waste a glance in her direction. *How incredibly rude,* Julia thought. It seemed to her as if in a split second her and Sura's roles had been reversed. Julia suddenly felt that she was here to protect Sura and to serve her slave, rather than the opposite. She stepped forward between Stephanus and Sura.

"The name *is* Julia. Julia Petreia, and I do not wish to be left outside."

"As you wish," he replied, finally looking at her.

Sura shot Julia an appreciative glance. The acrid fumes from the basins of urine assaulted them as they stepped into the atrium of the fuller's shop. In the small shallow pool, the impluvium, where rainwater collected, soda had been added and two female slaves were washing a long piece of gray wool. Aside from the water sloshing in the well of the impluvium, there were three vats immediately visible, and on a platform above them, smaller basins of urine and other rinsing liquids. The sounds of the stomping feet of perhaps half a dozen fullers could be heard as they trampled the fabrics in the treatment basins to soften them further.

Julia and Sura followed Stephanus toward a long table. Two slaves were at work on a piece of linen spread over the table. "Away! Away!" Stephanus flicked his hand at them as if he was shooing flies. "And careful how you roll that piece," he barked as they began to remove the linen from the table. Then he turned to Julia. "That cloth is for Popidius Celsinus, a supporter of mine for decurion. Might you mention to your father my campaign?"

Julia pressed her lips into a firm line and looked directly at the fuller before replying.

"Might I? Or *should* I?" As Julia spoke, she felt Sura stiffen beside her.

"Oh my goodness." He raised one thin eyebrow. It reminded Julia of a small leaping fish. *An anchovy*, she thought. "Do you study rhetoric, my dear?"

"No, I do not study rhetoric. Rhetoric is not a part of the curriculum for girls. Nor can females vote. Nor do men listen to women on such matters. So why would I waste my breath on a candidate that I do not know, for a vote I cannot give, to a father who will not listen?"

"My, my," Stephanus said.

But before he could continue, Julia stepped toward the table where two women had spread out the wedding fabric. "So when will this be ready? I must tell my mother."

Stephanus sighed and edged closer to the table and closer to Sura. Julia saw Sura flinch, and glanced down.

"Ouch!" the fuller cried out. His hand jerked away from Sura's bottom. A spot of blood appeared just beneath his elbow.

"Oh, my hairpin! So sorry," Julia said sweetly. She was holding the pin from the braid she had loosened. "Now, I think in five days we might have this back. Wouldn't you say so?"

"Yes, five days will be enough time," Stephanus said shortly. And then almost as an afterthought, he added, "I could deliver it myself. I have some other business to discuss with your parents."

Julia was confused. What possible business could this

man have with her parents? Was it regarding the election? She stammered, "That . . . that won't be necessary. I shall have my mother send Faustus for it. Come, Sura, we have much to do."

"What a vile, disgusting human being," Julia said as she and Sura sank back into the cushions of the litter. "Does he always do that?"

"Yes, except when his wife is around."

"Oh, he has a wife?"

"Yes," Sura sighed.

"Poor thing!" She paused. "I should lend her my hairpin."

Sura laughed. "Julia!"

Seven

DINNER WAS IN THE SUMMER
dining room, which opened onto the garden.
At last Cornelia and her fiancé Cassius would
occupy the place of honor on the middle
couch. On a second couch, the customary place for the
master of the house and his wife, Julia's parents were just
reclining. Opposite them, sharing the third couch, were
her cousin Marcus, his mother Livia, and her husband,
also named Marcus. Julia was late. She came rushing into
the dining room. Cornelia shot her a furious glance. *Foot!*
Cornelia mouthed. Julia quickly backed up, then stepped
forward, placing her right foot, and not her left, very de-
liberately over the threshold to avoid bringing bad luck. No
one else had noticed this violation of dining etiquette except perhaps for her cousin Marcus, who would think it
was funny. Julia then proceeded to a basin, where a slave

poured water over her hands. She removed her sandals, and another slave washed her feet.

"These sea urchins are simply marvelous," Julia's aunt Livia exclaimed, and helped herself to another as a servant walked by with a platter heaped with delicacies from the sea that included everything from the urchins to sardines and conger eel.

"Try the pullet, Livia," Cornelius said, and signaled a slave to bring over another platter with two young hens that had been roasted to golden perfection.

"And the dormice," Herminia added. "A new recipe—try and guess the stuffing." Roasted dormice were a staple of every Roman table. Julia liked to help the cook catch the dormice, who roamed in a fenced-off area of the garden.

Livia took a bite of one, closed her eyes, and thoughtfully chewed. "Minced venison and pine nuts?"

"Pork," Herminia answered. "Yes, and pine nuts."

"Delicious," Livia said, and then turned her attention to Julia. "How sweet you look, child. Now tell us what you shall wear for your sister Cornelia's wedding. You looked charming for Flavia's. I dare say you should wear the same stola, or at least that color. It so becomes you."

"No," Cornelia interrupted sharply. "She must look different for my wedding."

"What does it matter?" Cassius asked, and pinched Cornelia's cheek. "No one shall take their eyes off my beautiful bride." Cornelia tucked her chin in and giggled. Nestling up to her fiancé, she tipped her cheek so it rested on Cassius's arm. They were always nuzzling and saying completely inane things to one another. It made Julia want to vomit.

"Come sit next to me," her sister Flavia said. Flavia and her husband, Cuspius, were at the other end of her parents' couch.

Julia looked at her mother. "May I, Mother?"

"Of course, dear."

"There's more room over here," Marcus said.

"Oh, we'll fit her in," Flavia replied.

Julia blushed. "I'll be right across from you, Marcus— see!" And she plucked a grape and flung it at him. He opened his mouth and caught it. Everyone laughed. Julia walked over to the couch and wedged herself in between Flavia and Cuspius.

She liked Cuspius so much. He never spoke down to her but treated her as if she were the same age as her older sisters. Her aunt Livia, however, was occupying his attention completely. She was trying to wheedle out any information about the upcoming games for the Vulcanalia Festival. Julia found this conversation much more interesting than the endless talk about weddings. But she couldn't understand her aunt's sudden interest in the games. Aunt Livia was married to her father's brother, and there was often tension between her mother and Livia. They were about as different as two women could be. Her mother considered Livia "coarse," coarse in her looks—she was overly painted and as stuffed as a roasted thrush, as Herminia once said—and coarse in her conduct. Herminia also thought Livia put on airs. Julia agreed, and she often wondered how Marcus had turned out so nice and smart. She didn't think either her aunt or her uncle was very bright.

She looked at her aunt now and studied her. In spite of being fat, she was very pretty. Her kohl-rimmed eyes were sparkling now as she talked with Cuspius. The violet stola she was wearing matched the color of her eyes and set off her heavy necklace with its large chunks of gleaming pyrite and turquoise beads the size of hen's eggs. Her hair was dyed a violent shade of red, and her over-rouged cheeks gave her a rather hectic complexion. To Julia's eyes, Livia appeared almost encrusted with jewels and overly embroidered stolas and tunics. Her villa was the same. Every wall was painted with elaborate gilt-edged scenes, and she had a newly commissioned fountain of Apollo driving his chariot that was the talk of Pompeii. "Spends money like a fool!" Herminia would often mutter. Julia sensed it was not the money that offended her mother so much as the poor taste that Livia unfailingly demonstrated. The Apollo statue had been called tawdry and overdone, and Apollo was said to be cast in the likeness of her husband. Supposedly this helped Marcus Octavian part with the thousands of sesterces it had cost. But despite all this, Julia still liked her aunt Livia quite a bit.

"So," Aunt Livia said to Cuspius, "is . . . now, what is his name? Oh my goodness. Things just fly out of my head these days." She tapped the elaborate coils of braids as if to jostle her brains. "You know, my dear—the retiarius who fought so beautifully at the Neptunalia games." A retiarius was a net fighter. His weapons were a net and a trident.

"You mean Gavianus?" Cuspius replied.

"Yes! That's the one. What a fine fighter. A beautiful fighter!" she said dreamily.

"Yes, he shall be fighting. I can't tell who he'll be against. But the roster of fighters is a good one. That lanista from Rome, despite what they say about him, does get good gladiators."

"But such a repulsive trade," Herminia said, sucking on the bone of the pullet. "Trading in human flesh, really, isn't it?"

"No agents, no games, my dear," Cornelius said. "Old Tullius gave us over a decade of wonderful gladiators. It's a hard business. You buy, you sell, you rent. You have to come up with twenty good pairs of gladiators for every feast day, not to mention the games to honor dignitaries, or for important funerals. Then you have to maintain them, take care of them. That was what was wrong with Gaius Rufus. Now *there* was a degenerate man if there ever was one. The human flesh he wasted!"

"They ran him out of town finally, didn't they?" Cornelius's brother Marcus said.

"Yes, and it was good riddance."

The main course had finished and slaves began clearing away the dishes. Sura and another slave girl came with loaves of bread, which were broken and then passed around for wiping mouths and hands. Cornelia summoned Sura, and as the slave bent over, she sneaked a wipe of her greasy hands on Sura's long thick hair.

Julia felt Flavia wince. It was terrible behavior.

Julia looked at Sura and, as she so often did, wondered if it bothered her. How was one to know a slave's mind? And she was close to Sura, closer than any mistress ever was to a slave, or so she thought. But still she knew there stretched between them a vast gulf that was truly uncrossable.

"Cornelia does it to irritate me," Julia whispered, glaring as her oldest sister again covertly wiped her hands on Sura's glossy long black hair.

"Attention!" Livia was raising her glass as if to offer a toast. She then looked at her husband. "Marcus?"

"Yes," said Marcus. "We have a little announcement to make."

Julia glanced at her cousin Marcus. The color had drained from his face.

"As many of you know, our son Marcus has been promised to Drusilla Maximia since he was five years old and she was four. This month on the same day as the lovely Cornelia and Cuspius are joined in marriage, Marcus turns fifteen. By Roman law he will be a man. We, too, have been consulting with the augurs and the haruspices and have now fixed a date for the wedding of Marcus and Drusilla."

"You have?" Marcus croaked.

"Yes, it is to be on the seventh day of October, my son. And the formal betrothal will be in one month."

"My sponsalia in a month?" Marcus seemed in a daze.

Everyone began to applaud. Julia, though, was as stunned as Marcus. Yes, she had known that Drusilla and he had been betrothed since they were very young, but somehow she never expected the marriage to actually happen. How had he grown up so fast that he could now marry?

"The seventh day?" Marcus said. "That's less than two months from now."

"Yes, yes, dear—plenty of time," Livia replied. "It's really the bride's family that has all the work to do, as I am sure Herminia will agree."

"Oh, yes!" Herminia nodded.

"So I say," the senior Marcus continued, "let's raise our cups to young Marcus and his future wife."

As cups were raised to be quaffed in one swallow, which was the custom for toasting, Julia slid her eyes toward Marcus, who looked completely bewildered. She had to get them out of here. Her mother often excused them early from the table. She would ask just before dessert was served. By that time everyone would be fairly tipsy.

It seemed like forever before the platters of dessert began arriving.

"Mother, might Marcus and I be excused to walk in the garden?"

Livia gave Marcus a sudden sharp look. "No! Marcus is no longer a child. He is soon to be married. He should remain at the table, not go toddling off with Julia."

Toddling off with me! What am I, a baby? Julia was furious. She had always thought her aunt Livia liked her.

"Mother!" Marcus began to rise from the couch.

"Livia, don't be ridiculous!" Her husband patted her hand. "Let them have a turn in the garden. Here, have some more wine." He poured the remainder of his cup into his wife's. "He has the rest of his life to be a husband." He sighed and everyone laughed. Everyone except Julia and Marcus, who quickly got up to leave.

"Did you know this was going to happen?" Julia asked Marcus as soon as they were at the very farthest end of the garden.

"No, but I should have suspected something. I do turn fifteen in less than three weeks and . . ." His voice dwindled off as they walked through the night shadows that stretched across the garden.

"It's not the end of the world," Julia said, and then immediately regretted it. "Oh, I am so sorry. I didn't mean to say that. That was terrible of me."

"No it wasn't. The thing I love about you, Julia, is that you always say what you think. You are the most honest person I know." He paused. "It's not the end of the world." He paused again and looked deeply into Julia's eyes. "But it is the end of something, isn't it?" He took her hand, her limp, dead hand. Marcus, aside from Sura, was the only person with whom Julia was not self-conscious about her arm.

Julia felt the color rising in her face. She was not exactly sure what he meant by these words, or how to respond. "But Drusilla is a sweet girl and so pretty," she said. He was still holding her hand, and now he squeezed it gently. She did not have much sensation in those fingers, but she could feel a little, and it both excited and confused her. Was it pity he was showing her, or something else?

"Yes, I suppose so."

"She's a cousin on your mother's side, isn't she?"

"Second cousin." Marcus let go of her hand.

"But, Marcus, we'll still be friends. We'll see each other all the time."

"Yes, but it won't be quite the same, will it?" Marcus's clear gray eyes looked questioningly at Julia. The color of his eyes had always fascinated her, and she loved his high broad forehead and the way his very straight brown hair fell across it. She had told him once that he should never let a tonsor make curls for him, and he had laughed.

He smiled now. "You must really be tired of wedding talk—and now mine."

"Sick to death of it!"

"But when your time comes—" Marcus started to say, but Julia interrupted him.

"Don't be ridiculous!" She decided to change the subject quickly. "Tell me, Marcus, why does your mother have this sudden interest in the games?"

A sly smile crossed Marcus's face. "Now, why do you think, Julia?"

Julia looked hard at her cousin. "I'm supposed to know?"

"Think!" He barely suppressed a chuckle.

"She's in love with a gladiator?" Julia whispered the words.

"Yes, of course," Marcus replied, his eyes glittering.

"Who?"

"Gavianus, who else?"

"But she could barely remember his name."

"That's part of the ruse. Julia, for a smart girl you are so innocent!"

"Does your father know?"

"I assume he doesn't. They have very separate lives, really. They enjoy different things. Still, I don't think he would be pleased. No man would be. And my father is not really very confident. I mean, your father is clearly more successful. He's now a member of the ordo. Cornelius Petreius is a hard older brother to live up to in many respects. But to be cuckolded by a gladiator . . ." Marcus paused. "Well, you know what I mean." Julia nodded. "And," Marcus continued, "Gavianus is a wonderful gladiator. You'll see him at the Vulcanalia games."

"I can't wait for the Vulcanalia," Julia said. "I hope Mother isn't too caught up with the wedding and doesn't make us all come home as early as she says she will."

"If she tries to make you leave early, you can stay on with us."

"Well, that might work," Julia replied. She knew that her father greatly admired Marcus, and she often wondered if he would have traded some of his daughters for a son like her cousin.

The laugher from the dining table was spilling across the garden now. Someone had probably told a bawdy joke. That was usually why Herminia let Julia leave the table early. She didn't really approve of such joking, but she knew all too well that as the evening progressed and the wine flowed it was inevitable, especially when her husband got together with his younger brother. And Livia was as raucous and lewd as any of them.

Julia and Marcus had settled down by the far end of the pool near the Venus fountain.

"Look," Marcus said, running his hand under the spout. "It's hardly flowing."

"You're right," Julia replied.

"You know, it's odd. The public fountain at the square was hardly running either when we came."

"Really?" Julia replied. "I wonder what's happening."

"It could be small cracks in the aqueduct, the great one, the Aqua Augusta, or one of its branches. It's happened before."

"When? I don't remember."

"Before you were born. Before I was born—the earthquake seventeen years ago."

"How do you know about it then?"

"My old tutor explained it. It didn't happen all at once, but pressure builds up underground, deep in the earth. It's as if the foundations of a building are shifting and tiny, minute fractures begin. They fixed those old ones in the Augusta, but maybe they didn't do such a good job. I'm sure that if this is starting to happen throughout the city, the chief engineer, the aquarius, will look into it."

"Julia!" Marcus said suddenly. "Smell this!" He lifted his wet hand to her face.

Julia wrinkled her nose. It was the same sulfurous odor that she had smelled that afternoon at the mouth of the Sarnus. Like rotten eggs.

A shadow slid across the garden walkway.

"Who's that?" Julia asked.

"Me!" Livia giggled and swayed slightly. "Came to apologize for my remark." She turned to Julia. "Your uncle is right. Marcus has the rest of his life to spend with Drusilla."

Marcus's face darkened. There was a tension in the air that had not been there moments before.

"Yes," Livia continued. "And it's so nice when cousins are close. I shall speak to Drusilla about you being an attendant at the wedding, Julia."

Julia shut her eyes. *Oh, by the gods, not again!*

"You'll do no such thing, Mother. Drusilla is perfectly capable of selecting her own attendants."

"Oh, now, Marcus, when you get that grumpy expression you look so much like your father!" She waved dismissively, turned, and teetered back the way she had come.

Julia looked at Marcus. "What was the meaning of all that?" She nodded toward Livia, who almost stumbled against the urn where Sura had put the apricot pits the night before.

"I don't know. I don't know." Marcus shook his head wearily.

Eight

SURA COULD HEAR JULIA'S EVEN
breathing. Usually this rhythm made her
sleepy, but tonight she felt wide awake. For
days now a fear had gnawed at her. At first
she tried to dismiss it. She had told herself countless times
that she had heard wrong or perhaps misinterpreted what
she had heard. But tonight there was no mistaking the terrible words she had caught after she left the tablinium. This
was the room was where all the family records were kept
and where the master of the house conducted his business.
Sura had been summoned to bring an extra oil lamp and
a jug of wine. When she entered, she was surprised to see
both master and mistress there poring over the accounts.
Undoubtedly studying the figures for the upcoming wedding of Cornelia, she thought. They had dismissed Sura after she set down the wine and lighted the extra lamp.

Something about the way that both the master and mistress were regarding her as she lit the lamp had sent a shiver through Sura's entire body on this hot night. The flame of the squib had trembled in her hand so hard that she could barely hit the wick with it. If it hadn't been for the way they were looking at her, she would never even have thought of trying to listen in on her master and mistress's conversation. But when she left the room she lingered in the shadows outside the tablinium, which was at the back of the interior courtyard. The tablinium was only separated from the rest of the house by a wooden screen. It was easy to hear. Their voices carried. Especially the mistress's, because she was once more becoming agitated. At first Sura thought it was the same old argument.

"You say there would be enough for a twenty-thousand-sesterces donation to the temple. That is wonderful, Cornelius—enough to reconstruct the roof and lay a new architrave over the south-facing pillars."

"And the wedding wine. Falernian," the master added.

"Yes, yes, of course. We can't have Falernian for Flavia's wedding and not Cornelia's. It would look terrible. And so unfair. Cornelia is difficult enough." She paused before continuing. "And you're sure he said he will pay more than half in advance and the rest after the wedding?"

"Yes, that is part of the agreement. It is due in three days."

"It's wonderful, really." But her mistress's voice did not sound as if it were brimming with joy. Then there was a deep, weary sigh. "I can't help but be worried about Julia. She won't like it. Sura has been with her since she was born. And he's such a coarse man."

Sura felt her heart skip a beat. Her breath locked in her throat. This was not just about the Temple of Venus. This was not just about the wedding. It was about her—Sura. The scene in the fullery came back. The moment when Stephanus said that he would bring the wedding cloth himself, that he had business with Julia's parents. Not just her father—that would have perhaps been about the election. But he had business with *both* Julia's mother and father. That could only mean one thing: they were selling Sura. The women of the households were always consulted on such domestic matters as the buying and selling of slaves, for it was the women who had to keep the home running smoothly. And now they would have enough money for the finest wines to serve their guests at Cornelia's wedding and for the reconstruction of the Temple of Venus. It was all perfect.

Sura was suddenly hit with a realization: she was not human. She a commodity no different from a slab of the highest-grade marble or a barrel of the best wine. She was flesh to be traded. Her head began to swim. She felt her legs grow weak. They were not selling her to just anybody. Stephanus the fuller would be her new owner. And clearly she was being sold to be not just an ordinary slave but a concubine. She was sure of this. Why else would Herminia be sighing about this man being so coarse? What would she care if Sura was only going to pummel cloth in vats of urine in the fullery and not share his bed?

Her life had begun to change on that day in late June when she had delivered the cloth for Flavia's wedding clothes to be cleaned. Stephanus, reeking of the urine that was used as the cleaning agent, had leered at her when she handed over the cloth. He began making all sorts of inquiries that had nothing to do with the business of preparing Flavia's wedding clothes. How long had she worked for the family? Did she serve one person or was she just a general household slave? This was not the kind of information anyone really needed. When she had returned for the cloth a few days later, he had tried to pinch her breast. But she had been too quick for him. Then a few weeks later, Sura had caught snatches of conversation between the master and mistress that had begun to worry her. It was nothing definite. There had been no specific names mentioned. Not hers, not the fuller's. She only knew that they were discussing money and that references had been made to the price a slave could fetch on the open market versus a private transaction. But now the pieces of this diabolical puzzle fell into place. And the cold hard truth stabbed like a sliver of ice into her heart. She was being sold for three barrels of Rome's finest wine and a roof for the Temple of Venus.

Sura lay on her pallet feeling dazed. This was the only home she remembered. Both she and her brother Bryzos had been captured when a Roman legion had swept down on their mountain village in Thrace, setting it on fire. After catching them both in nets, the Roman soldiers had bundled Sura and Bryzos aboard a cart filled with other young girls and boys who would fetch a good price at the slave markets. They were lucky in only one respect—they had both been bought by citizens from Pompeii. Bryzos, who was nearly seven at the time, was purchased by Aurelius, a lanista, who would train him for the gladiatorial contests. Sura was purchased by Flavius Cornelius Petreius to serve as a slave to his soon-to-be-born child, which he hoped would not be another daughter. Although Sura was not quite five, he could tell at first glance that the Thracian child would serve quite well—she was clearly strong and quick-witted.

The family of Cornelius Petreius had been good to Sura. She had been taught to read and write by the family tutor, for she would be expected to help the child with lessons in the future. The mistress was extremely beautiful and vain, but still kind. There was never a harsh word from either the mistress or the master. Indeed her only nemesis was the cook, a cantankerous crone named Obliata who shrieked at everyone. This life was all she had really known. Her memories of Thrace, of her mother and father, her grandmother, had grown dimmer and dimmer with each passing year. She was comfortable here, and although Julia often talked about manumission, giving her her freedom, it really hadn't mattered to Sura as long as she could stay with Julia and be near her brother, who lived in the gladiator barracks. She was able to see him often. Household slaves were allowed to go freely around the city and even carry money. It was necessary, for there were always many errands to run for their masters and mistresses.

Freedom to Sura was still a rather vague notion. She had never really thought about it that much. What did it matter if she was not paid? She had everything she needed here in the home of Cornelius Petreius. But now Sura began to think about freedom and what it could mean, and slavery and what it really meant. Her life was not her own at all. She could be sold like the barrels of wine her master would buy for Cornelia's wedding. She would honestly rather endure a flogging of one hundred strokes, she who had never even felt the lash of the whip for one stroke, than be sold to that disgusting fuller Stephanus. But did it really matter whether it was Stephanus or someone else? She wanted to stay here.

Sura sat up on her pallet. Would she dare run away? The punishments for runaway slaves were brutal. She could be thrown to animals in the amphitheater, or have a foot chopped off, or be sold into a brothel. As a brothel slave, she would be made to lie with men, dozens of men, every day.

The high whine of the town crier slipped through the shadows as he turned into their street. *Media noctis inclinatio.* It was midnight. The day of Mercury had already turned into Jupiter. There was no time to waste. Sura peered into the darkness. She had to see her brother now. Bryzos would know what to do.

Five minutes later she had dressed and was in the street on which the villa Petreius fronted. She turned the corner and cut diagonally across a square, avoiding the thermopolium on the opposite side, where the rowdy voices of late-night drinkers tumbled into the night.

The moon was nearly full, and as Sura raced across the Forum, her own shadows stretched over the travertine slabs, mingling with those of the statues of generals and emperors, of gods and poets. In the center was the altar of Augustus, both god and emperor—the first god-emperor after the fall of the Republic. Now every emperor was a god. But not every god was an emperor, Sura thought suddenly, and wondered if perhaps these gods that the Romans worshipped and sacrificed to so lavishly were still nonetheless jealous of the new emperor-gods.

Once across the Forum, she threaded her way through a series of alleys and emerged on the Street of the Theaters on the west side of the Triangular Forum. She was approaching the neighborhood of the gladiators and the gladiator barracks. The graffiti that was scrawled all over the walls of Pompeii now had one subject: the celebration of gladiators. "Celadus the Thracian is the glory of the girls," one bit of writing exclaimed. "Twenty pairs of gladiators furnished by Valens the glorious will fight April 8 through 12." "Greetings to Gavianus, slayer of beasts, and hearts!"

Then she heard a woman laugh, and in the moonlight there was a gleam of turquoise and pyrite. She knew that necklace; it belonged to Livia Octavia. Livia was just coming out from one of the doors of the barracks, and she was accompanied by her slave. They were heading directly toward Sura. Plastering herself against a wall, she pulled her palla so it covered her face, but she could still smell the heavy jasmine scent that Livia always wore. Pressing herself flatter, she hoped that she would simply merge with the darkest of the shadows. Livia Octavia swept so close to her that Sura could have reached out and touched her. But the woman was giggling hard now with her slave, and neither one noticed her. When they had safely gone by Sura entered the barracks through the door from which the women had just left.

Turning down a corridor, Sura tapped lightly on the first door. She waited, and then she knocked harder.

"Who's there?" a groggy voice called out.

"Me, Sura."

The door opened. Her brother's dark hair was tousled. He blinked at her. "Sura, what is it?"

"I am to be sold."

He pulled her into his small room.

"You cannot run away. It is unthinkable, Sura." Her brother had not ceased holding her hands tightly in his during the entire time Sura related her story.

"The man is awful, Bryzos."

"It won't be that awful. You say he wants you for his concubine. He will never beat you unless you stray to another man." Although he was trying to keep his voice calm, Sura noticed that he was rubbing his sword arm as he spoke, which was always a sign that he was tense. Bryzos was a murmillo. He fought bare chested with only a short sword, helmet, and shield, and his arm protected by a manica of linen.

"He won't beat me unless I stray to another man. So I am never able to choose in love."

"You are a slave. That is what being a slave means."

"You are a slave, too, Bryzos, but you have been able to choose in love."

"I am a gladiator; that's different. And besides"—there was a bit of a sly twinkle in her brother's eye that was not lost on Sura—"I don't get to choose, really, I am chosen."

Sura thought of Livia Octavia choosing Gavianus. But still she knew that her brother had had many girlfriends that he himself had chosen.

"This is not the worst fate." He spoke in a soft voice.

"Think of Julia," Sura pleaded.

"Julia, why should I think of Julia? She's a rich, privileged brat."

"She is not a brat, and I am all she has known. She is used to me."

Sura shut her eyes tight as if to will this whole night away.

"Look, Sura." Bryzos put his hand on her shoulder. "Your life has been good compared to many slaves."

"I know, Bryzos, and that is what is going to make this all the harder. I don't want to leave."

"Have they settled on a date for Cornelia's wedding?"

"Yes, the twenty-fourth day of August."

"But that's Mundus Patet," Bryzos said. "She wants to get married on the day the doors to the underworld open?"

"The mistress has been consulting every augur in Pompeii. They must have been telling her that this was not a good date. But Cornelia is stubborn."

"Well, I really doubt that you will have to leave until after the wedding. They will certainly need you and will not want to upset Julia before it's necessary."

"But it is August tenth. The wedding is only two weeks away!"

"Things can change in two weeks. Deals fall through. Maybe Stephanus will find another slave he wants, a prettier one." He looked at her sister with a sly sparkle.

"If you're trying to appeal to my vanity, it won't work," Sura said stubbornly. Her eyes became stony and her angular jaw had a defiant set.

"Listen to me, Sura." Bryzos leaned in close to his sister and took both of her hands again. "Look at that wall." He nodded toward the wall by a table. "How many palm fronds do you count?"

Sura counted silently. "Fifteen. You have won a new one since last time I visited."

"Yes, up the coast in Misenum. The admiral of the fleet, Pliny himself, presented me with it, and something else." Bryzos got up and pulled his bed away from the wall. He took out a short knife and wedged it in between two bricks, which came loose, then reached his hand into a hole in the wall.

"Look at this!"

A pile of gold coins glittered in the palm of his hand. Sura gasped. "How did you get these?"

"Pliny gave them to me."

"You have started to receive money for your wins?"

"Yes, and more." He went to a cupboard, unlocked it with a key, and took out an ornate sword inlaid with precious stones. If gladiators were awarded the winning purse, even though they were slaves, they were permitted to keep it. The payment was established beforehand. The lanista, of course, got a cut. But when the combat had been particularly spectacular, the victor was often awarded something beyond the agreed upon amount, and the lanista had no claims on that additional award.

Sura turned the sword over in her hand. "This is amazing."

"The jewels alone are worth eight thousand sesterces," Bryzos said.

"Eight thousand! That's almost half of what Herminia Petreia needs for the roof of the Temple of Venus."

"Exactly!" He bent down over his sister, who was sitting, and took her face in his hands. "I am becoming a rich man. A few more contests and I shall be able to buy my freedom, and then I shall buy you from that disgusting man, Stephanus the fuller. You could stand him for a short time, couldn't you, Sura?"

"I suppose so. But what if he won't sell me?"

"He'll sell. Believe me, that man has a reputation for greediness. Monumental greed. He is obsessed with money."

"And young girls, I guess."

"Don't think about that."

But Sura was not thinking about that. She was thinking about what would happen if Bryzos didn't win. Then what were her hopes of freedom. *Freedom?* How curious, how bizarre that she had never even really thought about that word before, and here she had been a slave for almost twelve of her sixteen years.

On her way back home, Sura decided that she must go to the Temple of Jupiter and make a sacrifice on the eve of the contest. If her brother was going to buy her back, he was going to need a lot of money. But where could she get the money even to buy a chicken for the sacrifice? Perhaps Julia could get one for her. But then she would have to tell Julia the whole story. Or she could just say that she was worried about her brother fighting. Surely that would be enough.

By the time she settled onto her pallet at the foot of Julia's bed, the town crier's voice could be heard again announcing the first hour of the last segment of the night. *Finis noctis diluculum! Finis noctis diluculum.* One more hour until dawn. And then *hora prima*, the first hour of the day. Already she could hear the master's clients gathering in the street at the door of the villa. The house had begun to stir. She looked up at Julia sleeping so peacefully. Her strange arm hung over the side of her bed. How awful that because of this arm her destiny was fixed. *Perhaps she is no more free than I am.*

Nine

JULIA STOOD ON A SMALL PEDESTAL as the seamstress draped the stola over her shoulder. The cloth was rich, richer than what she had worn for Flavia's wedding, and she became suspicious. In the few days since the announcement of the date of Cornelia's wedding, several things her mother had mentioned about her participation in the celebration—even the fact that an ornatrix would arrange her hair and not just the bride's—had aroused her suspicions. But now this lavish cloth with the richly embroidered palla made her suddenly alert.

"Why so fancy?" Julia asked.

"My dear," her mother replied, "I wanted it to be a surprise, but you are to be a bridesmaid for Cornelia."

Julia was stunned. Usually only married women served as bridesmaids. "Does Cornelia know about this?"

"Of course. It was practically her idea."

"Practically?" Julia said, and darted a fearful glance at Sura. Had Sura known about it? Sura shook her head.

"But what about Valeria? Valeria is Cornelia's best friend."

"Valeria will be Cornelia's pronuba," Herminia said. The pronuba was the most important bridesmaid. "And Flavia will be a bridemaid. But Cornelia really wanted you to be one, too."

Julia's suspicion deepened. "Why, because I shall never be a bride and never again be able to dress so richly?"

"Don't be ridiculous. She wanted you because she loves you. She cares about you."

This was such transparent nonsense that Julia did not even deign to answer. But she was wary. Some plot was being woven. A design was being put into motion. It was almost as if she could hear the first squeaking turns of the cogs.

The next day Julia's wariness increased when it was announced that the family auspex would be paying a visit that morning and her presence would be required. Sura delivered this news.

"This is crazy, Sura. Something's up."

"No, mistress. You mother says that it is required that the youngest bridesmaid meet with the family auspex before the wedding."

"She just made that up. I never heard of Flavia's youngest bridesmaid, Camilia, doing this when she got married. Camilia never came to meet with our auspex."

"Well, maybe he went to her house instead," Sura protested weakly. "Anyhow, you are to go to the lararium immediately."

Five minutes later, Julia, with Sura at her side, entered the lararium, where the longtime family auspex, Tiberius Calpurnius Maius, smiled benignly at her. Cornelia had already arrived and seemed to be regarding her with an expression Julia had never seen before. Her oldest sister was studying her carefully. Was there almost a shadow of regret in her eyes, a hint of worry?

There was no chicken in sight, but Julia felt a cold fear begin to steal through her as she spied the circular woven container. *Snakes, no!* Julia hated snake offerings. She did not simply find them revolting. It was more complicated. Their eyes in particular, unlike those of chickens, seemed to possess a certain intelligence. Julia detested the way a dying snake's eyes fastened onto you in the course of the sacrifice. It was as if they were reading you rather than the reverse. And Tiberius was so old and palsied he did not handle animals for sacrifices well. They wiggled around and often got away. He needed his attendants for anything larger than a chicken, like a ewe or a pig. But a snake! Why a snake? Julia had never heard of a snake being offered in connection with any wedding rituals.

On the morning of the wedding, the auspex came early and would perform the official sacrifice to the household gods. If the auspex deemed the entrails of the slaughtered animal favorable, this signaled that the marriage ceremony could begin. But why, Julia wondered, was Tiberius here today? Was this really something to do with her being the youngest bridesmaid? He hadn't come before Flavia's wedding day. Why now? And who was the woman who stood in the shadows? A priestess, but not just any priestess. Her green stola and lighter green palla indicated that she was a damiatrix, a guardian of the Temple of Damia. The worship of Damia—also called the Bona Dea or the Good Goddess—a patroness of fruitfulness of the earth and women and of healing, was considered a somewhat new religion in Pompeii. Her mother had nothing but disdain for these newer cults imported from the east, even though this one was closely associated with the worship of Venus.

The lives of the damiatrices were closely modeled after those of the vestal virgins in Rome. They rarely left the precincts of their temple, which was on the outskirts of Pompeii. Virgin girls between the ages of eight and fourteen were chosen for service. The service of the damiatrix, like that of the vestals, lasted a period of thirty years, during which time they were required to remain virgins and forbidden to marry. If they violated this pledge, the punishment was the same as the one for the vestals—they would be buried alive. To have a daughter selected to be a damiatrix brought much honor to a family, just as it did to have a daughter chosen to be a vestal. Yet although it was associated with the healing arts and medicinal herbs, there was one aspect of the organization that Julia found absolutely loathsome: snakes, albeit harmless ones, were permitted to slither about freely within the confines of the temple.

"What's she doing here?" Julia whispered to Sura.

"I have heard it is a recent practice. It is supposed to bring fruitfulness to the marriage."

Julia shrugged. Her parents had not had a damiatrix anywhere in sight when Flavia had married. The only thing she could figure out was that their mother feared the date of August twenty-fourth, so she had decided that extra help was necessary.

The auspex came forward and kissed Julia on each cheek, another thing he had never done before. His breath smelled of garlic, and the stench of wine reeked from his pores. He was a drinker, there was no doubt about that. And at any wedding, by the middle of the feast, he usually had to be removed by his attendants.

"Julia, my dear, how you have grown. A veritable young lady!" His face turned white, and beads of perspiration stood out like dewdrops.

Tiberius began with an invocation to the family gods, the lares, and to the penates, the minor household gods who were responsible for keeping the larder full and free of vermin and minding the door of the villa. He then called for his attendants to come forth with the basket containing the snake. Tiberius nodded toward Julia. Her eyes opened wide.

"Me?" she murmured. But before she could reply, the damiatrix was by her side, and she felt her hand being taken by the slightly puffy and moist one of the woman in green. She slid her eyes to look at her. The woman stared forward and did not acknowledge Julia in any way except to continue holding her hand.

The lid of the woven box was opened and the old auspex reached inside and took out the snake. It was the most common kind used for readings. The snake, a fat old fellow who seemed more dead than alive, hung from Tiberius's hand. One of the attendants handed the auspex the knife. The old man's hands were trembling as he took it. Julia settled her eyes on the mask of her great-grandfather and prayed that old Tiberius would make a quick business of it and not slice off his own hand in the process. But in the midst of her silent prayer, a sudden hissing cut like a blade through the air. And this time it was not the eyes of a dying snake that terrified Julia but those of a living one. The snake had coiled up around the auspex's hand and was lashing out directly at Julia's face. Its diamond head jabbed toward her as its forked tongue licked the air just inches from her eyes. There were screams, and Julia tried to step back, but the damiatrix had locked her forearm around Julia's narrow chest, and she could not move either backward or to the side.

"Let me go!" Julia screamed, and wrenched herself free just as the head of the snake was sliced off.

"Don't worry, dear," the auspex was saying. "It meant nothing."

Julia wheeled on the damiatrix. "But what did *you* mean?" she seethed. "Why were you holding me? What does all this mean to you?" Julia was enraged.

"It wasn't a poisonous snake," the damiatrix replied. "You were in no danger."

"That's not the point. It has fangs. They are sharp. Their tongues can hurt, and it was striking at me, right at me."

"Oh, no, Julia," her mother said soothingly. "You must be mistaken. It couldn't have been striking at you. The snake was blind."

Blind! The word exploded in her head. *Blind, and yet it chose to strike at me. Was it an omen?* That was Julia's last thought before she fainted.

Ten

WHEN JULIA REGAINED CONSCIOUS-
ness, she was in her bed. On one side of her
was her mother, looking quite worried, and
on the other side was Sura, who looked in-
describably sad.

"Are you all right, dear?" Herminia asked.

"Not really," Julia replied.

"It was just a ceremony that is done sometimes before a
wedding—a new one, I admit, but it is supposed to insure
fertility."

"Whose? Mine?"

Julia's mother gasped in dismay.

"The snake seems to have confused the bridesmaid and
the bride. And how come this was not done before Flavia's
wedding?"

"All the signs for Flavia were more propitious. You

know the problems we have had with this date. It's Mundus Patet, after all."

"Well, I hope this does the trick for Cornelia, because it certainly scared me half out of my wits. I hope she has dozens of babies!" Julia spat the words. Every syllable was laden with disgust and scorn. To herself she thought, *Dozens upon dozens of squalling, ugly, puking babies.* And she hoped that Cornelia would get enormously fat in the process. She herself had had it with being the younger sister of brides. If she never saw a bride or a wedding again it would not be too soon.

Her mother stroked her forehead. "Now just rest, dear. Sura will get you some wine." Her mother kissed her and went through the door. Sura followed her to fetch the wine.

After they left, Julia began to suspect that what had transpired in the lararium had nothing to do with fertility or Cornelia and her marriage. A dark fear began to invade her. It spread until she felt far worse than she had when the snake had coiled and begun to strike out at her. Why had they brought a blind snake? Julia had never heard of a blind snake or any blind animal being used for a ritual. The animals used by auspices and sibyls were all supposed to be perfect.

"I don't want any wine!" she announced as Sura came through the door with the jug. "Just water." Her mind needed to be clear. Julia knew that she had to think this through and could not let fear get the best of her. She looked up at Sura, who still wore a look of profound sorrow. It struck her that Sura had in fact looked this way for several days now, and she had simply not really been aware of it.

"Why are you looking that way, Sura?"

"What way, mistress?"

"You look sad and you look frightened."

"It just gave me a scare with the snake, even though it was not a poisonous one. That's all."

"No, that's not all. You actually look more than frightened and sad, you look . . ." Julia searched for the word as she studied Sura's face. ". . . distrustful."

"Distrustful, mistress?" This took Sura aback.

"Not distrustful of me. But you . . . you suspect something, don't you?"

"Oh, no, mistress. No. No."

She is answering too quickly, Julia thought. *Too quickly.*

"Sura, I don't think that ridiculous ceremony had anything to do with Cornelia and her marriage. Have you ever heard of a blind snake or a blind anything being used by an auspex or a haruspex?" Her eyes drilled into Sura's. A blade of sunlight pierced the slatted shutters and slid across Sura's olive face as she looked down to the floor.

"No, mistress. Never."

"What do you make of it?"

Sura hesitated, then sighed. "Slaves are not asked to make anything of anything. We do not have opinions, mistress."

Julia jumped from her bed. "By Pollux that is not true, Sura. You know that as well as I do. We have shared everything. I ask you all the time what you think of this or that. I asked you what you thought of Cornelia's fiancé Cassius, and you said you thought he was a bit arrogant—and not so bright, as well you said. All these years I have asked and you have told me what you thought."

"Yes, mistress," Sura answered, her eyes now filling with tears.

"What's wrong? Why are you crying? And quit calling me 'mistress.'" Julia's voice suddenly softened. "Sura, you are my best friend. You know that. I have promised to free you when I grow up. What is wrong with you? It's not just what happened in the lararium. You have been this way for days. Sad. So sad." Julia paused. "You can't say it is nothing. It is something. Can't you tell me? I have told you that I don't think that the ritual with the auspex had anything to do with the marriage of Cornelia. It was about me, wasn't it?"

"Perhaps."

Just perhaps? She knows more, Julia thought. "Tell me, did they open the snake and read the entrails after I fainted?"

"No, mistress, I mean Julia, no they did not."

"See? So what was the point?"

Sura shook her head slowly. "I . . . I don't know."

Julia really didn't know what worried her more, Sura's sadness or the mysterious ritual that had just taken place. It was all too odd. The sound of the cogs turning, the machinery of that fearful design, was becoming louder in her mind.

Eleven

"NO, MOTHER, IT SIMPLY WON'T do," Cornelia whined. "It must be a heavier fabric. Anyone can see through it in spite of all that embroidery. They'll be able to see her arm. The cloth is almost transparent."

"Cornelia," Flavia barked. "That is so cruel. It doesn't matter. The color becomes her. The drape is lovely. And it is such a beautiful cloth. Think of the money your father has spent on it. It can't go to waste."

"I'm sure I could use it. It could be part of my trousseau."

Herminia squeezed her eyes shut as she spoke the next words. "You are so selfish."

"No, Mother, I just want what's mine."

"This is not yours. This is the fabric picked out for Julia, and I won't hear another word about it."

Julia stood on a pedestal in her mother's dressing room

while the seamstress snipped and clipped the peach-colored silk with its fine embroidery. *Why do I have to be going through this!*

"Can I resign?" Julia asked suddenly.

"Whatever are you speaking of, Julia?" Her mother stood up straighter and adjusted a pin in her braided coronet. "Resign from what?"

"Resign from being a bridesmaid." Everyone burst out laughing, including the slaves and the seamstress.

Herminia came up to her youngest daughter and pulled on her hair playfully. "Magistrates resign, darling, city councilors resign, sometimes even senators, but bridesmaids? Oh, how curious you are!"

"A bit too curious with that arm!" Cornelia fumed.

"Cornelia, we've had quite enough of that."

"But, Mother, you didn't allow her to wear such a transparent material for Flavia's wedding. It's simply not fair!"

"It is fair!" Herminia spoke sharply. "It's much much hotter than it was when Flavia got married. Do you want the poor child to boil to death?"

"I should be so lucky," Cornelia muttered.

With that Flavia rushed across the room and slapped her older sister. Julia leaped down from the pedestal, knocking over the seamstress, and delivered a swift kick to Cornelia's backside.

"Girls! Girls!" Herminia shrieked. The slaves stood

back, their hands pressed against their mouths to conceal their laughter.

"What in the name of Jupiter is going on in here?" Cornelius burst into the room. By this time Cornelia and Flavia were wrestling on the floor, and Cornelia was pulling Flavia's hair. One of her hairpieces flew off. *Oh, this is fun,* thought Julia. *This is worth being a bridesmaid.* She was attempting to stuff the hairpiece in Cornelia's mouth.

"You horrible creature." Cornelia's words were muffled by the hair.

"Yes, one bad arm, you monster, but see what I can do with the good one!" she screamed at Cornelia's flushed and stuffed face. The hair foamed out from Cornelia's mouth like a rabid dog's spittle. But then Julia felt herself being lifted into the air by a slave. Another slave was separating Cornelia and Flavia. Herminia stood transfixed. She was mumbling something about the augurs' warnings about this wedding.

"Now, what is this about?" their father boomed.

"It's about Julia's dress," Cornelia shouted.

"You don't have to shout." Cornelius lowered his own voice as he said this.

"It is not about Julia's dress," Flavia said with a quiet dignity that caught her father's attention. "It is about Cornelia's cruelty to Julia."

Cornelius Petreius's large blue eyes opened so wide they

were like huge fathomless pools in his face. He wheeled about to face his eldest daughter. "It is about her arm. Well, Cornelia"—he took Julia by the shoulders and pulled her toward Cornelia, and then lifted the long sleeve that was covering the deformed arm—"look at this hard, my dear. Get used to it."

"Why?" Cornelia said. Her bottom lip was trembling, and Julia had never seen her so scared, nor had she ever seen her father so angry.

"This might be the Curse of Venus, or it might not."

Julia gasped. Finally those words had been spoken, spoken by her own father. This cut deeper than anything Cornelia could have said. Julia's eyes filled with tears.

"But whatever it is, it's a curse that has been visited before on our family."

"It has?" Cornelia said, her voice quaking with fear now.

"What?" Julia said.

"Cornelius!" Herminia interrupted and then hissed at her husband. "Don't speak of such things."

"I will if I have to, Herminia."

Julia was stunned. She had never heard this before, and she could tell that neither of her sisters had either. A flood of joy swept through her. She was not completely alone. She was not the first person in the family this had happened to. And perhaps she was not such a freak.

Cornelius then turned to Julia. "Now, child, enough of all this wedding nonsense. Come with me. I have to go to the Forum on some business and then we shall go to the harbor. And how would you like to go to our favorite restaurant and have ourselves some octopus? What do say you to that?"

"Oh, Father, yes."

"And I think we'll go by the jeweler and find something precious for you to wear for the wedding. You are a bridesmaid, are you not?" He turned his head toward Cornelia. "And you shall be properly honored. I think jade, yes. I saw a lovely jade piece at Lucretius's."

"Jade!" Cornelia was quivering with anger.

"Yes, jade, Cornelia," her father replied coldly. He began to walk out and then stopped and turned toward Cornelia. "Cornelia, you are about to be married. You have so much. Jealousy is unbecoming to anyone, especially a bride. Make some space in your heart for love."

Julia watched her sister. Tears had begun to spill down her cheeks. These were tears not of anger but of sorrow and regret. "I am sorry, Julia," she said quietly. Had Cornelia ever before in her life said these four words?

"Let's walk to the Forum, Julia. The sun's not high yet. This is the coolest part of the morning." He turned to the two slaves who stood by the litter. "Lido and Servius, meet us there in one hour with the litter and then we shall go on to the port."

As they turned onto the street, there were the usual

petitioners calling out for favors. These were not the official clients who were permitted into their patron Petreius's house, but just gangs who hoped something might be tossed in their direction. Julia and her father hurried by them. As she had been trained to do, Julia walked quickly with her eyes straight forward.

Every few feet, storekeepers came out to bid the magistrate good day and inquire if he would be purchasing from them for the next wedding. The wine merchant ran to him in the street.

"Will it be the Falernian, Flavius Cornelius Petreius?" the merchant asked, using his patron's full name as a sign of respect.

Petronius laughed. "I'm afraid so, dear fellow. I wish it on no one—two daughters' weddings in one summer."

The wine merchant pinched Julia's cheek. "But a while until this little one. Don't worry, your father shall buy the wine of Falernian for your wedding, too!" Julia pulled her palla tighter over her arm and heard her father cough nervously. This wedding was like a stray hungry dog that seemed to follow them everywhere. It was impossible to get away from it!

Soon they were at the Forum. "Father, when will your statue be put up?" Julia asked, glancing about at the statues of the dignitaries and emperors that lined the immense rectangular space.

"Soon, my dear."

"Where will it go?"

"Over there between Pliny's and that of Eumachia, perhaps."

"Are Eumachia and the empress Livia the only statues of women in the Forum?"

"Yes, a priestess and a goddess." But the word "goddess" was tinged with disdain. Julia knew that although her father was no Republican he looked askance at the deification of the emperors and especially the empress Livia, wife of the great Augustus. She was rumored to have been a consummate poisoner who had succeeded in poisoning two of her own sons and several grandchildren.

"Will your statue be sitting on a horse?"

Cornelius laughed heartily. "Julia, my dear, the very idea! I would undoubtedly fall off even as a statue. I am no general. I am a merchant, a shipbuilder. Better to put me on the deck of a bucking trireme than a horse. Come along now. I have to clear up some business details."

The business details that Cornelius Petreius was required to attend to in the Forum had nothing to do with shipbuilding. He was one of a pair of senior magistrates called duoviri to whom the maintenance of sacred and public buildings as well as the roads was entrusted.

Julia and her father mounted the steps of the building that was the center of these activities. A half dozen scribes sat behind stone desks with their styluses and wax tablets.

"Ah, Januarius, is my dear colleague Quintilius Pomponius in?"

"Yes, sir."

"Good, good. I'll see him right away. Could you fetch us some figures on carrera marble, including shipping and installation?"

Julia followed her father into a spacious room. A rotund man sat at a desk. He was bent over a wax tablet, so Julia could see that his partially bald head was inscribed with a perimeter of perfectly fashioned curls. The curls reminded Julia of flattened snails. She once again thought of Marcus's hair and how it fell so naturally across his brow.

The man looked up and smiled. "What a pleasure! You have brought my absolute favorite Petreius daughter, the lovely and clever Julia." Quintilius Pomponius was the other magistrate who served with Julia's father as one of the duoviri. "Come have a most fabulous fig while two boring old men talk business."

A slave immediately materialized, carrying a plate of not just figs but large purple grapes, peaches, and apricots along with a small jug of peach wine.

"So what is it, Cornelius?" Quintilius Pomponius asked.

"Well, I believe that I have secured enough money to begin reconstruction on the Venus temple, from a source that shall not be mentioned,"

"Aaah." Quintilius Pomponius laughed slyly. "I bet I know who that source might be."

This was the first time that Julia had heard this good news. She supposed now her mother and father would stop squabbling about it. That hadn't taken long—what, only twelve years or so?

"I am having Januarius fetch some figures for materials—carrera marble and installation."

"For the pillars perhaps, but you'll have to go with travertine for the floors."

"Yes, I suppose so," Cornelius said, rubbing his chin.

Quintilius Pomponius now cleared his throat. "I am afraid, dear Cornelius, that there is right now a more pressing matter." The seriousness in his voice alerted Cornelius as well as Julia. She loved being included in this talk. *A serious matter, not a wedding matter—how refreshing!*

"Did you happen to pass by the public fountain near the thermopolium two streets over?" Quintilius Pomponius asked.

"No, I'm afraid we did not come that way," Cornelius said.

"Tell me then, how are the fountains in your own garden?"

"I think quite normal."

"No, Father," Julia piped up. *By the gods, why did I say that?* She and Sura had sneaked out to go swimming again and had noticed this second time that barely a trickle flowed from the Venus fountain.

"What is that, Julia?" Both men turned to her expectantly.

"Well, Father, the other night, I could not sleep—you know, when it was so hot?—and Sura and I took a turn in the garden." *Well, that was true.* "And we noticed that the shell of Venus was almost dry. No water at all. But by morning there was some."

"Curious." Cornelius looked at Quintilius Pomponius. "Of course, my wife prefers that the pressure be maintained at its very lowest on all the fountains in our garden. She finds loud splashing or even just dripping disturbs the tranquility."

"I think it's a real problem, though." Quintilius Pomponius's brow contracted into deep furrows.

"Well, we had better contact the aquarius."

"Yes, I have sent word already."

Julia wondered if she should mention the odor she and Marcus had sniffed that evening when the fountain was barely running, the smell of rotten eggs. But her father and Pomponius were already on to other matters.

By the time Cornelius Petreius's business at the Forum had been concluded, the sun was high and the heat of the late morning lay on the city thickly. It turned all the marble statues into quivering and seemingly insubstantial masses. The rays of the sun's light struck like shards of glass. Julia squinted her eyes against it as they walked to where the litter with the bearers awaited them. The darkness of the litter's interior was a welcome relief, and her father pulled out a jug of cool water from which they both drank, a practice her mother would have frowned upon and said was for "road slaves." Julia settled back into the comfort of the linen cushions. These bearers were among the strongest and the smoothest runners of her father's slaves. It was almost as if the litter was floating along a swift river current. She relaxed and time passed quickly.

"Here we are, Julia. Your favorite restaurant."

Aurelius Josephus, the owner, came out to greet them. He was a Jew. "Ah, Cornelius Petreius!" He opened the door of the litter and began welcoming them effusively while directing his own slaves to make a table ready.

"No, no need for a table. My daughter Julia here prefers to eat at the bar."

"Of course, of course!" He quickly showed them to the stone bar with holes in which amphorae of wine were set. Julia's father ordered all of the specialties—the octopus, conger eel wrapped in beet root, salad with many lettuces, a platter of sea urchins, oysters, and boiled crawfish.

"Tell me, Aurelius Josephus"—Cornelius winked at Julia as the plates began to arrive before them—"how does a Jew like yourself explain serving shellfish? Doesn't your religion forbid the eating of such creatures?"

"I don't eat them. I just have my cooks prepare them. Simple enough."

"But does it disturb you to see others eating them?"

"Why should it disturb me? You have your gods, I have mine."

"Just one, right?" Cornelius asked, sucking the juice from an octopus tentacle.

"One's enough for me. One god. One wife. That's it." He slapped his hands together. "And what, may I ask, is the occasion that brings you and your lovely daughter to my humble restaurant?"

"She is sick to death of all the foolish wedding talk. As am I."

"Oh yes, and you have to pay for it all."

"Indeed I do!" Cornelius said as Aurelius Josephus filled his glass with more wine. "That reminds me, can you get me a good deal on a barrel of these oysters? They're delicious."

"Of course I can. What's the date?"

"August twenty-fourth, just a week away."

Aurelius Josephus went and fetched a wax tablet. With his stylus he wrote down the order. "The day after the Vulcanalia. Good you got your order in now. I'll deliver them at dawn on the day of the wedding. Anything else you need?"

"Flamingo tongues, but they're not exactly your department."

"Oh, Father, I hate flamingo tongues," Julia said, making a face.

"Well, it's not your wedding, and your mother and Cornelia want them." Cornelius was getting out his pouch to pay.

"Try them with a little garum," Aurelius Josephus suggested. "The sauce helps. They'll taste just like tuna."

I doubt it, Julia thought. But she thanked him nonetheless and said she would do just that.

An hour later, on the very opposite side of the city from the port, Julia looked at her wrist. The circlet of jade disks was beautiful, each one a slightly different color green. "Father, I love it! I just love it. The stones have every color of the sea," Julia exclaimed.

Her father laughed. "Well, I'm a shipbuilder not a sailor, and I have not seen every color of the sea, but it becomes you, Julia." He gave her shoulder a squeeze.

They had just climbed back in the litter and her father had ordered the bearers to carry them out through the gate to the necropolis and their family's tombs. He had bought a jug of the peach wine they had drunk at lunch as an offering.

More than a quarter of a hour later they came upon the small stone house of the dead where Julia's ancestors' ashes rested. They passed through the open entryway into the cool shadows of the building. Urns containing the ashes were placed on shelves and then beneath these shelves were strong boxes containing clothes, jewels, and various possessions the deceased had used in life. Julia always went first to the urn that contained the ashes of a small child, a girl named Paulina who had died during the time of the Republic, nearly one hundred years before. She often wondered what Paulina's box contained—toys undoubtedly, but from the inscription, Julia could see that the child had died so young she did not have enough years to collect many favorite things. Julia felt the weight of the jade bracelet on her own wrist and wondered if when her time came it would be buried with her in a strongbox beneath her ashes.

She had a sudden thought. This girl Paulina had lived during the times when children like herself who were born with deformities were often taken to hillsides outside the city and abandoned to be devoured by wolves or to die of starvation.

"Father, if I had been born, say, one hundred years ago, would you have carried me to a hillside and left to die?"

Cornelius Petreius gasped. "Julia, what a terrible thing to say or think about. Of course not. Never!"

"But, Father, that was the custom, was it not? And some people still do it?"

"Those were very brutal times."

It wasn't much of an answer in Julia's mind. If they were brutal times, did that make the people naturally brutal?

Would her father have been born brutal then? Or could he have made up his mind not to be?

"But it was the Republic. Many say that those were Rome's finest hours."

"Republicans! Now, don't go talking such nonsense. Come, let's leave."

"Father, you haven't made your offering."

"Oh, yes—yes, of course."

Julia took a bit of wine from the jug, cupped it in her hands, and dribbled it over the urn of the long-ago child Paulina. In brutal times, did it follow that a child was born brutal? These were not such brutal times, yet Cornelia was brutal. How had that come to be?

All the way home they were quiet. Julia was absorbed in her thoughts of abandoned babies. She tried to imagine what it was like for such a baby. Did the baby smell the breath of the wolves as they approached? Did it know enough to even be frightened? Or was the baby just feeling hunger and cold? Did it take long for it to die? That would perhaps be the worst. Suppose the wolves didn't come, and the baby just cried and cried into the darkness of the night, the broiling heat of the day, the emptiness of this world into which it had been born. Even if it did not know enough to be scared, and even if it did feel cold or hunger, what must have been the worst was the emptiness, the complete loneliness of the universe. The loneliness would have been crushing. One didn't have to be smart to feel loneliness. One only had to be human. Of this Julia was sure.

They reentered the city by the Vesuvius Gate. There were tombs near this gate as well, and beyond the tombs closer to the base of Mount Vesuvius there was a refuse heap where the trash and garbage of the city was taken. It was to that refuse heap that she might have been taken had she been born a century before, or even possibly in this century to different parents. Her father sat on her left side, the side of her withered arm. With her right hand she picked up the limp left one and slipped it into her father's. He squeezed it slightly. She could not squeeze back. She turned her head toward the mountain. It was massive and seemed to glower under a white sun. Its flanks covered in vineyards were bleached as gray as bones in this heat. The snow that crowned its top in winter was all gone and had been since early March. *Take care, my dear, and remember as hot as it is now, when snow comes in summer that is the time to leave.*

The words of the Sibyl of Sarnus. Julia had not thought of them since that day. Well there was certainly no snow coming this summer. Julia wished she could squeeze her father's hand, but instead she leaned her head against his shoulder and closed her eyes. *Some things will never change. Never,* she thought.

Twelve

 "I TELL YOU, HERMINIA, THE CHILD has a morbid turn of mind."

"Now just what do you mean by that, Cornelius? Stubborn yes, but morbid never."

"Well, do you know what she asked me the other day when we went out?"

"What?"

"She wanted to know, if she had been born a hundred years ago would I have exercised my patria potestas, and as father abandoned her on a refuse heap."

"By the gods where does she get these morbid thoughts indeed?"

"Yes, not only that, but when I offered that those were brutal times, she went on to say—and to quote your daughter—"

"Our daughter," Herminia said sharply.

"Our daughter," Cornelius Petreius continued. "She

said—I believe these were her exact words: 'But it was the Republic. Many say that those were Rome's finest hours.'"

"By Venus, it must be that tutor Remigius. I knew he was a Republican the moment I first laid eyes on him. Well, that's finished now, thank goodness. Have you written to him yet, Cornelius?"

Sura's eyes widened in fear. It was all beginning to make perfect sense. Perfectly awful, horrid sense. On the day Julia had gone out with her father, the lady in green, the damiatrix from the Temple of Damia had appeared and spent long hours in a huddled conversation with the mistress of the house. But could this really be true? Was Julia actually being given to the Temple of Damia? What else was there to do with an unmarriageable girl? The vestals wouldn't have her because of her deformity. However, these newer religions or cults were perhaps more lax. And the stature of the Bona Dea and her temple was growing in Pompeii. It was considered an honor to be part of it. And now Sura caught her mistress saying just that word.

"I know it's considered an honor now, but . . . but . . ."

"But what, Herminia?" Cornelius asked. "You must remember that there is security for her as well. She is the youngest. She will never marry. They will take care of her into her . . ." His words dwindled off.

"Old age?" Herminia's voice broke.

"It's a better way," Cornelius replied firmly. *Better than what?* Sura wondered.

"I know, I know you're right." She made a sound that Sura thought was either a gasp or a chuckle. "It's just hard imagining Julia ever old. She's so young and full of life."

"But look at Claudia Plautia's life," Cornelius Petreius said with an intensity Sura had never heard before from her master. "She has no deformity such as Julia's. Yet she's attracted all sorts of miserable people who try to get money from her. Remember how you hated going to her villa with those people? And now no one of any consequence will go there. She is a lonely old woman, smart about business and stupid about life."

"Julia would never be stupid in that way."

"Of course she wouldn't. And she's smart about many things. She, of all our children, is the most apt student. She will learn a lot about herbs, medicines. The temple is becoming a center of healing superior even to the temple of Rome. This is truly an honor, Herminia."

There was a terrible logic to all of this, a brutal logic, Sura thought. Once Julia was at the temple, she would no longer need a slave. Thus, she herself was being sold to the fuller Stephanus.

Sura had been standing behind a tall hedge of cypress in the enclosure where the dormice roamed. She had been sent by Obliata, the cook, to fetch a half dozen. Preparations for the wedding now just three days away had begun in earnest, and although Sura rarely helped in the kitchen, she was now called upon to do so into the long hours of the night. She stood clutching the jug in which six mice scampered around, most likely wondering what they were doing in this dark airless place that smelled of clay and not clover.

Sura had begun to tremble, but she willed herself to be calm. She had to think of something. Julia would die in that temple crawling with snakes. But what could she do? She was a slave and had no more choice about her own life—let alone Julia's—than these dormice had about what would happen to them in the next few hours as they roasted on spits. Gripping the jug tightly, she looked at it, hearing the dormice's tiny panicked squeaks, the frantic patter of their feet. *How odd,* she thought, *Julia and I both, mistress and slave, are as trapped as these mice.* She had a sudden urge to set them free, but what would that get her? A slap by Obliata, and another slave would be sent out to fetch some more. What had been a vague notion, that of freedom, burned with a new intensity. She felt herself almost glow with the possibility. Freedom, she realized, had nothing to do with getting paid. It had nothing to do with the fact that until ten days ago she had felt her life was comfortable. The truth was that it was not her life at all.

"Well, my dear," the master was now saying to his wife, "despite your criticism of Livia you must say that in this one respect she was quite helpful."

"Yes, and one can hardly consider it a cult in the least, not if Appuleia Messalina contributes. And it is true, Livia's mother was cured by that damiatrix and not Gaius the Greek, who has even treated the emperor."

"And don't forget Quintilius Pomponius was treated by her as well. I think the day of the Greek physician or the Jewish one might be ending." Cornelius chuckled. "Our daughter will be a healer, and really, Herminia, as I have said, she is the brightest of them all. So we should thank Livia for her help with this. It was a substantial contribution that she arranged for Marcus to give to the temple in appreciation for healing her mother. Usually she is trying to wheedle money from Marcus for jewelry. And this donation certainly made the damiatrix more inclined toward us and Julia."

"Yes. Well, I'm gratified that Livia was the one who made the initial approaches. The damiatrix is a bit odd. I don't think I would have been comfortable with her in the beginning." Herminia paused. "My only real objection to Livia, aside from her minor vulgarities, is that she tends to be promiscuous in terms of the gods and goddesses. So many of the temples she is connected to are these new cults from the east, not true religion. All that Isis nonsense from Egypt. Oriental mysticism is not part of the Roman pantheon! But the Temple of Damia, I admit, seems different."

Livia! Sura thought. *I must contact Marcus.* She was not sure what Livia's son Marcus could do, but he was very smart and he loved Julia dearly. He would be shocked to hear this. And he must be told.

Thirteen

"WHAT'S IT WORTH TO YOU?" the squat, burly night porter asked Sura as she stood in front of the gate that led into the villa of her master's younger brother on the Via degli Augustali. She knew it would come to this. The night porter was a swinish fellow who was always pinching slave girls' bottoms. A pinch she could stand, but she had a feeling he expected more.

"Well, I'm not certain." She cast her eyes down. He hooked a finger under her chin and pried it up so that she would look him straight in the eye. His eyes were squinty, slightly tilted. *Yes, exactly like those of a pig.*

"Well, you should be certain, I think."

"A kiss?"

"Just a kiss?"

"More later, if you can get me in to see the young master."

He looked at her slyly. It was said that pigs were intelligent. But this man's eyes swam with stupidity. A kiss would do. Let him catch her for more. She tilted her chin up higher and looked him brazenly in the eyes now.

"Yes or no. I can't stand here all night!" she demanded.

"Yes!" He suddenly seized her and smashed his face against hers. He was gristly and smelly and Sura gasped when he stuck his tongue in her mouth. She pulled away abruptly.

"Now let me in."

He opened the gate and Sura entered and threaded her way through a narrow tunnel-like entry into the atrium. Unlike her master's house, the bedrooms were not on a second level but grouped around the atrium. Walking by one room from which snores issued, she guessed that it must be the master's bedroom. The mistress's was most likely next to this room with a connecting door. At the very end was a third door. It must be Marcus's. She tried the door. It was not locked, and praying it would not squeak, she opened it as narrowly as possible and slipped through the slender space. An oil lamp with a low wick cast a flickering light across the room. The figure of Marcus appeared lumpy under the covers. His face was turned away from the door. Sura had taken off her sandals as soon as she had entered the house and now tiptoed to the other side of the bed.

She stood looking at him for a moment. In the pulsing lamplight his eyelashes cast spiky shadows on his cheeks.

How should I wake him? she wondered. If she startled him too much he might shout out. She bent low and began to whisper into his ear. "Marcus. Marcus." She repeated his name five, perhaps six, times. His eyes opened, not suddenly, but then he inhaled sharply as he saw her.

"Sura!"

"Shhh!" She held a finger to her lips.

"What are you doing here?"

"It's terrible." Her heart was racing so hard it felt thunderous in her chest. "It's about Julia." She wanted to add that it was about herself, too, but that was not why she was there.

"What? Julia? Is something wrong?"

"Everything!"

He sat up in bed. "What is it? Is she sick?"

"No." She looked at him steadily. "She is going to be given to the Temple of the Bona Dea."

"Damia?" Sura nodded slowly, keeping her eyes steady. "How do you know this?"

She began to explain. When she had finished, he was still for what seemed a long time and then looked at her gravely. "And you are sure of this, Sura?"

Nodding, she began to tell the part of the story that involved her. "I am to be sold to Stephanus. To be his concubine. You see, Julia will no longer need me. It is all very neat, isn't it?"

A cold look crept into Marcus's usually warm eyes. She knew that he was convinced.

"By Jupiter!" His voice was hot with anger. "My mother has gone too far with her damnable cults, and this one especially, ever since my grandmother was supposedly cured by that damiatrix." But there was something else that he was not saying, and yet he was certain—his mother wanted to get him away from Julia. She had guessed that their cousinly affection was turning into something more. What better way to put an end to that than to get Julia away? But he would not say this to Sura.

"Mistress Herminia says it is not a cult but a religion."

"It's a cult, believe me! And only the gods know what they do at that strange place with their roaming snakes and potions." He looked directly at Sura. "You say that nothing will happen until after the wedding of Cornelia?"

"Oh, I am sure of that. They need me too much, and Julia's to be a bridesmaid."

A cunning look flashed in his eyes. "I have an idea."

"What?"

"Do you know my mother is seeing Gavianus the gladiator?"

"I do, sir. I saw her coming back the other night from the barracks when I went to visit my brother. But what does that have to do with any of this?"

"Simple. I shall tell her two things. First, that I will tell my father about about her trysts with the gladiator if she does not prevent Julia from being given to the Temple of Damia. If my father finds out, he will immediately cut her allowance. And second, if she does not stop Julia's entry into the temple, she can be sure that when my father dies, if she survives him, I shall cut whatever is left of her allowance in half. No—more than half. I'll cut it by two-thirds. She loves her jewelry more than any temple, believe me. This is not going to happen."

"That's blackmail, isn't it?"

"It most certainly is. But the worst thing that can happen to my mother is that my father will cut her allowance. She will not be able to spend her usual fifty-thousand sesterces per year on those stupid jewels. Now you tell me, what is worse, that my mother foregoes her necklaces and bangles or that Julia is sent to the Temple of Damia?" He paused and looked at Sura. "And that you are sold to that whoremonger Stephanus?"

Sura was almost speechless. She had not expected this at all. He was concerned about her. He was making her almost an equal to Julia. "Thank you, Marcus." She pressed her lips together. She did not want to cry.

"Now don't tell Julia anything at all. The day after to-morrow is the Vulcanalia and the day after that the wedding. Hopefully I can sort this out by the time of the wedding, or at least shortly thereafter," Marcus said.

"Yes. I cannot thank you enough."

"This is what's right. One should not have to thank anyone for what is rightfully theirs."

Does he mean one's freedom? Sura wondered. *Whose freedom? Julia's? Mine? Both?*

"One other thing . . ." Sura said.

"Yes, what is that?"

"I do not wish to leave by the front entrance. The porter . . ."

"Oh, that lecherous old man!"

"Yes."

"I can show you a back way out through the baths. The door is locked from the inside." He swung his legs out of the bed. "Follow me."

Sura walked out into the night air. It was odd how quickly things could change. She felt real hope now for the first time in days. Marcus truly was an incredible boy—no, he was a young man. He would turn fifteen on the day of the wedding. She wished Julia could marry him. According to Roman law, cousins could marry, but he was already betrothed. To break an engagement, although not against any law, violated all kinds of social traditions and brought shame to the family of the party who was responsible.

The stars had broken out and the peak of Vesuvius shimmered strangely in the moonlight. Sura did not feel tired at all. She decided to go to her brother at the barracks. He would still be awake. The gladiators stayed up late and tended to nap during the heat of the day when it was too hot to train.

She had just rounded the corner and was at exactly the same spot as on the night when she had seen Marcus's mother. Only this time it was not Livia Octavia that she spied. It was a wall inscription written with a broad brush in red paint, an edicta munerum, the program announcing to the public the contest in the amphitheater for the Vulcanalia. "Twenty pairs of gladiators will fight at Pompeii. No public moneys shall be used." Her eyes ran down the list. Two-thirds of the way down she lifted her hand to her mouth in horror. Gavianus the retiarius would fight Bryzos the murmillo. The retiarii fought with nets and tridents, a style said to be inspired by fishermen. Gavianus was a superb net fighter. Not only had he never been defeated, he had hardly been bruised. He was wily, brutal, and extremely precise with his net.

"It simply can't be! No!" Sura murmured to herself, "No! Not Gavianus!" She turned and headed back to the villa of her master. She could not bear to face her brother. *Yes, how quickly things can change,* she thought again as all her hopes seemed to melt away. Even the stars appeared to grow dimmer, and against the blackness of the night a weird baleful light emanated from Vesuvius.

Despite the heat, Sura felt a shiver run up her spine. She wrapped her palla tighter and hurried home. All the way she noticed that piles of kindling for the Vulcanalia bonfires had been stacked, even though the festival was still two days away. The nights at this time of year had become longer, swallowing up the light of the dawn. So although it was early morning when Sura finally returned to the Villa Petreius, it was still pitch black.

Fourteen

THE NEXT NIGHT JULIA DREAMED of a deep cave where the fire god Vulcan lived, belching his flames across the earth. The flames scoured every living thing—animals, people, plants, trees. People and creatures ran in desperation while the god's thousands of fiery tongues licked the earth. Nothing escaped except the fish. *The fish, the fish. If I could only turn myself into a fish I could swim down the Sarnus River into the sea.*

Sura was lost in her own frightening dream. On the pallet she clenched her fists tight. She was standing weaponless. Bryzos was beside her, and advancing on them both was Gavianus. She bent down pick up a handful of the sand from the arena. He laughed at her.

"You think that will stop me girl—a bit of sand thrown in my face?" There was a roar of laughter. The laughter grew. It was like thunder rolling across the amphitheater.

And still Gavianus advanced. The net he carried was huge, just like the one that had captured Sura and Bryzos those long years ago in Thrace.

That terrible day came back to her now in this dream. *I have no weapon,* she screamed silently in her dream. *No weapon!* But the words remained stuck in her throat. And then suddenly she saw that Bryzos had no weapon either, no shield, no sword. The net began to descend on them. The trident glared. *We are going to die!*

Sura and Julia broke out of their dreams at nearly the same time.

"Did I hear you cry out, Sura?" Julia asked.

"Maybe. I was having a bad dream."

"I as well. What was yours?"

"I dreamed that my brother was fighting Gavianus in the games today," Sura said.

"Oh, dear. He's supposed to be quite good. But you know if you dream something it usually doesn't come true."

"Oh, this will," Sura replied.

"How do you know that?" Julia asked.

"I know it because I saw it."

"In a dream, Sura."

"No, not in a dream, Julia. It is on the inscriptions of the edicta munerum. It announced that Gavianus the retiarius would fight Bryzos the murmillo."

The color drained from Julia's face. "Oh, no!"

"Yes." She dropped her head.

"I shall ask Mother and Father if you can go to the games with us since he is fighting." Julia paused.

"But slaves aren't allowed to attend the games. They will never let me go, especially not the day before the wedding. There is too much to do."

"They've been very good to me lately. And Father bought me the jade bracelet. I think they are trying to please me so I'll be a stupid old bridesmaid." Julia noticed an odd look flash across Sura's face. "Why are you looking at me that way? Haven't you noticed how they have been favoring me lately?"

Sura lowered her head. "Yes, it is so." She spoke in a barely audible whisper. Julia peered closely at her and once again saw sadness in her face. That profound sorrow had been like a shadow clinging to Sura's being for days now.

"Well." Julia gave her head a shake and her curls that had been pinned for the night fell down. "I shall ask nonetheless. Let's light the Vulcanalia candles. It is almost time to get up anyhow."

On the eve of the Vulcanalia the household had gone to bed early, since they would all rise well before dawn the next day in candlelight. Such was the custom.

"But you see, Mother, it is her brother, her only brother, and he is to fight against the undefeated retiarius Gavianus. She's so worried, Mother!" As soon as Julia had heard stirrings from her parents' rooms she had come to ask. "You must let her attend and sit with us. I want to be near her." Julia hesitated. "You know, if something should happen."

"Must?" Herminia raised a perfectly plucked eyebrow as she spoke to her daughter through the mirror. Julia hated these "mirror" conversations as she called them, the two faces alike but so different, the reflections of mouths moving but the sound coming from elsewhere. Her mother was beautiful and perfect. She raised both her creamy plumpish arms now to hold several braids while the ornatrix, the hairdresser, secured a pad beneath them to form a conelike confection on top of her head called a tutulus.

"What's this?" Julia's father entered the room.

"Oh, Cornelius, how handsome you look!" Herminia exclaimed. "But no curls?"

"You know I think they are ridiculous, Herminia. Our divine emperor Augustus never went in for such foolishness. He kept his hair trimmed simply. Didn't have to be chased about all day by a tonsor fussing with his comb and oils and perfume."

"Well, you look handsome all the same, my dear."

And he did as he stood before them in his perfectly draped toga, the hem of which was edged in purple. The purple could only be worn by senators, magistrates, certain officials, and priests.

Cornelius Petreius turned to look at his daughter.

"Why so glum, dear Julia? This is your favorite holiday, I thought, even more than Saturnalia."

"Father, Sura's brother Bryzos is scheduled to fight today against Gavianus."

"Gavianus, you say."

"He is undefeated, Father."

"Well, so I think is Bryzos," said Cornelius.

"But Gavianus has more experience."

"Now, Julia, just because I am the sponsor of these games, I cannot change who fights whom."

"No, Father, I am not asking that. I just want Sura to be able to attend with us. It is her brother. She is so nervous. I would like her to sit with us. She was having bad dreams all night."

"Oh dear, wouldn't want that." Cornelius's brow creased. "Well, it is against the rules. But in this case, I see no problem."

"No problem, Cornelius!" Herminia wheeled around on her stool. "Do you forget that tomorrow we are having a wedding here? We've been shorthanded in the kitchen ever since Fabia died. We need all the hands we can get."

"Herminia, I think given certain circumstances"—he nodded knowingly at his wife, and Julia watched him closely—"we could permit it this one time."

"What circumstances?" Julia asked.

"Oh, nothing really, dear." Her mother laughed nervously. She then composed herself. "Yes, I suppose you are right, Cornelius." Julia had never seen her mother capitulate so quickly in an argument with her father. It was almost as if they were speaking in some kind of code.

"But I don't think Sura should go to the temple with us for the throwing of the fish. She should stay and help in the kitchen," said Herminia.

"Oh, she won't mind, Mother. Thank you so much. She'll be very pleased."

She ran up to kiss her mother and then hug her father. He seemed to squeeze her a little harder than usual. Almost as if he was not going to let go of her.

The Temple of Vulcan was outside the city walls. The fiery god was considered too dangerous to be allowed within the city itself. It was still dark when the Petreius family in two litters passed through the Forensa Gate. Julia unfortunately rode with Cornelia.

"I think I should have been permitted to go with my fiancé," Cornelia muttered.

"He'll be there, won't he?" Julia asked.

"Yes, with his whole family, and Julia, you'll meet many of his cousins and aunts for the first time, so please keep your arm covered."

No, I plan to wave it around in front of their faces, you stupid cow! Julia wanted to say. But instead, she just sighed loudly and said, "Don't worry about it, all right."

"Don't take that tone with me!"

"What tone?" Julia looked at her sister boldly, but Cornelia turned her face away and stared out into the dark dawn muttering something about "it can't happen soon enough."

"What can't happen soon enough? Your wedding?" Julia asked.

Cornelia turned her head. A slyness had crept into her eyes. "You'll see."

"What will I see?"

A suffocating panic welled up within Julia. She had that same feeling she had had a week ago when the snake had lashed out at her. Then there was the deadly terror that had engulfed her when she had regained consciousness after fainting. The terror came back. Her right arm, her good arm, which had enormous strength, darted about and gripped Cornelia's forearm. She sank her nails deep into the skin. Cornelia gasped. "Let go, you little rat."

"Tell me, Cornelia!"

"No."

"Cornelia, tell me. What will I see?"

"I can't. I promised."

"Promised who?"

"No!"

"Tell me or I'll . . . I'll . . ."

"You'll what?" Cornelia's lips curled back. She looked hideous to Julia.

"I'll bite you!"

Julia lunged at her sister's face, but Cornelia jerked away

just in time. At the same moment, the litter was set down, and Cornelia opened the door and exited without waiting for the slave to help her.

Cassius Marcellus was waiting for his betrothed, and beside him stood his brothers and sisters, several cousins, and grandparents. Many were meeting the Petreius family for the first time. Julia watched as introductions were made. There was a lot of commotion, and no one had noticed that Julia had let her palla slip off her left shoulder. The withered arm hung white and lifeless as a dead fish.

"And this is Cornelia's youngest sister," Cassius was saying, but he stopped in mid speech before he could say her name. A hush fell upon the group. They all stared at her arm. She stepped forward and smiled.

"I'm Julia," she said. There were a few nervous coughs. She stole a look at Cornelia, whose blue eyes had turned as cold as ice. *"You bitch!"* Cornelia mouthed. But Julia felt a kind of insane joy sweep through her.

"Well, let us get to the temple, now." Her father rushed them along.

At the altar cut from black rock, the flamen Vulcanalis, the priest of Vulcan, stood, about to begin his invocation to the dangerous and powerful god of fire. His white conical cap stood out darkly against the graying dawn. The hat was set in a laurel wreath encircling the priest's head, and atop the hat was a spike of olive wood with a tuft of wool tied to its base.

Julia's mother had pulled up the palla to cover Julia's arm and now stood beside her as the flamen came in front of the altar holding a large wriggling fish. He raised the fish high above his head.

"Vulcan Quietus Mulciber. In the name of Quietus, al-layer of fire, may our humble sacrifice quench the sparks of your devouring thirst. In the name of Mulciber, who charms the fire into beneficence for our hearts and homes, may you accept this fish and know that all the citizens of this city and of the empire are beholden to you for the things that we hold most dear." The priest then let out a wavering cry that scorched the air, and dropped the first fish into the flames. A cheer went up from the crowd.

"Julia! Julia!" She turned to see Marcus.

"Marcus, I am so glad to see you. I must speak to you!"

A look of alarm swept through Marcus's eyes. It startled Julia. "Why do you look that way?" she asked.

"What way?"

"You looked startled when I said I had to speak to you."

"Only because you appear so worried."

"I am, but we can't speak here." She turned to her mother. "Mother, can I go with Marcus and his family to the bonfires?" She had expected her mother to say no, but perhaps Julia's outrageous behavior of displaying her arm had made her mother want Cassius's family to see as little of her as possible.

"Yes, what a nice idea," she replied in a distracted voice.

"And we'll meet at the games," Marcus offered. For their families were all seated together in the special seats reserved for the most prominent spectators, which of course would include the entire family of Flavius Cornelius Petreius since he was not only a magistrate but a sponsor of the day's events.

Julia had a sudden and awkward thought. Aunt Livia would be there with them, cheering for the wrong gladiator, her lover Gavianus. Sura would be praying for his opponent, her brother. As far as Julia knew, Marcus knew none of this. She had to get away with him fast.

There was so much to tell, Julia did not know where to begin as they wound their way through the narrow streets to buy some live fish to throw on a bonfire. Such was the custom, as fish were believed to quench Vulcan's thirst for fire. They stopped near the restaurant where she had had lunch with her father. There was a bonfire there, and Aurelius Josephus the proprietor was selling live sardines. He welcomed Julia warmly and dumped a half dozen of the wiggling silvery creatures into a sack for her. Julia and Marcus then waited to get near the fire.

"I can't tell you everything here. Too many people," she whispered.

"I have enough money. I can hire a litter to take us to

the amphitheater in time for the games. That way we can talk privately."

"Yes, I need to talk. It's very scary." She looked up at Marcus. He was biting his lower lip, which he often did when he was nervous. "You know something, don't you, Marcus?"

He nodded almost sadly.

"Tell me."

"Make your prayer and throw the fish, and then we'll get a litter."

Julia reached into the bag and grabbed two squirming sardines. In her head she began to pray, but the words of the prayer were muddled. *I pray . . . I pray . . . by the gods I do not know what I pray for. Vulcan, you are the destroyer, but I feel my life is being slowly destroyed. What is happening?*

As soon as Marcus had made his offering, they set off in search of a litter. It took them a while to find one. When they did, Marcus promised the bearers a large tip if they would take the long way to the amphitheater and enter by the Stabian gates.

The sun was fully up now and it promised to be another blistering day. Julia had barely settled into the litter when she turned to Marcus. "Now tell me everything you know."

"First you must tell me what you know, and then I shall tell you what I know of it."

So she began by telling him what Cornelia had said to her on the way to Vulcan's temple. "There is more going on than simply Cornelia's wedding. I had this feeling before when the damiatrix came."

"The damiatrix from the Temple of the Bona Dea?" Marcus opened his eyes wide.

"Yes." Julia then explained about the ceremony with the blind snake and how she had fainted. Marcus picked up her limp left hand and stroked it quietly. "You see, Marcus, I had the same feeling then that this ceremony was not about Cornelia getting married or fertility. Is it somehow about me?"

"Yes. It is about you." Marcus said this steadily and looked her straight in the eye.

Julia gasped. "It is? I mean, how do you know?"

Marcus began to tell how Sura had come to him in the middle of the night, and what she had first overheard Julia's parents discussing. "Sura heard them talking about selling her."

"Selling her!" Julia turned white.

"Yes, she is to be sold to Stephanus the fuller, to be his concubine."

"What?" Julia gasped. She closed her eyes tight. Of course, that was why Sura had been so sad all these days. And then to hear about her brother having to fight Gavianus . . . But she had been sad long before she had heard about Bryzos fighting Gavianus. Why had she said nothing?

"It's true," Marcus continued. "But there is more, and

you shall see why this all makes sense. Even more sense now that I know how the damiatrix came to your house."

"Sense? How could any of this make sense?"

"I did not say good sense. It is a kind of, kind of . . ." Marcus groped for the right words. "A kind of horrible sense."

"What are you talking about, Marcus?" Tears trembled in Julia's eyes.

"Julia, you are to be sent to the temple to serve the one called the Bona Dea, a goddess of healing."

A small yelp escaped from Julia's throat. She crumpled over, curled her one good hand into a fist, and beat her knees. "No! No! No!"

"Julia, listen to me. It won't happen." Marcus took her head in both his hands and forced her to look at him. "I promise you it won't happen."

"How can you promise such a thing? You have no power to stop it."

"Yes, I do."

"What? What power do you have?"

"My mother has great influence with the Bona Dea. I was going threaten her by saying I would tell my father about her relationship with Gavianus if she did not get the damiatrix to refuse you as a guardian in the service of the temple. But I have an even better idea now. A wonderful idea."

"What's that?" The tears were streaming down Julia's face.

"Julia, I have always loved you. You know that. We can run away and get married."

"Married?"

"Yes married. Don't you want to marry me?"

Julia's heart was hammering in her chest. This all seemed impossible in so many ways, but it also made sense—good sense. *Love. I have always loved him,* she thought. Loved him in a way she had never realized until this very moment, and yet some part of her had always known. It was as if her heart had known but her head had failed to understand this until right now.

"Yes, yes! I love you!" she said with wonder and profound amazement. "I do!" She caught her breath. "But, Marcus you are already betrothed."

"Forget that. They can't make me marry Drusilla."

"But girls like me aren't supposed to get married."

"Girls like you aren't supposed to waste their lives in service to some cult, either. Julia, tomorrow is not only your sister's wedding, it is my birthday."

"I forgot."

"Yes, I shall be fifteen and by Roman law I will be a man. Also by Roman law a boy may marry at fourteen."

"But Marcus, although it might be legal, your father will disinherit you. I know it."

"I am his only heir. He won't. He knows his estate would then go to my mother and she would simply waste it with her spendthrift ways. He has already had to borrow from your father."

"He has?"

"Yes," Marcus said.

Julia, somewhat calmer, settled back against the pillow. A slight smile stole across her face. "We could have a double wedding with Cornelia. Imagine how she'd like that!"

"Julia, we will have to run away. No wedding, at least not a family one."

"But what about Sura?"

"I don't know. It's not really within my power to save Sura from being sold."

"Could she run away with us?"

"Don't be foolish, Julia. Then we would be guilty of theft. She is you father's property."

"Yes, I know."

Marcus looked out the window. They were approaching the amphitheater.

"Julia, listen to me now. We must attend the games as if nothing has happened."

Julia nodded solemnly. "But when should we run away, Marcus? Before the wedding? That is tomorrow."

"No, not before—during. By mid-afternoon the feasting will be well under way. By the time darkness falls everyone will be drunk. That is when we will leave. Be careful to drink no wine."

Julia looked at Marcus evenly now. "Marcus, are you sure?"

"I have never been more sure of anything in all my life. I love you. I love all of you." And he picked up her withered arm and pressed it to his lips.

Fifteen

SURA HAD A PERFECT VIEW OF the fat neck of Livia Octavia from where she was seated in the second row of the family box. She thought again of how awkward this would be—she and Julia cheering for Bryzos, and Livia undoubtedly hurrahing Gavianus.

The official parade, the pompa, had already begun when Julia and Marcus appeared. All the gladiators, including animals ranging from lions, bears, and cheetahs in cages to camels and elephants were marching around the arena led by musicians playing horns, tubas, and pipes.

"Marvelous musicians, Cornelius." Livia leaned across her husband to speak to her brother-in-law.

Hah, thought Sura, *it's not the musicians' horns she's after.* Livia Octavia was craning her head about now and rising from her seat to spot Gavianus as the double row of gladiator combatants approached. Julia turned around and gave

Sura a quick smile, then offered her a light sprinkling of perfumed water that Marcus had bought her to cool herself off. Sura shook her head no.

The music ceased as the parade came to a halt in front of the official podium. Cornelius Petreius stood up. As one of the sponsors, it was his duty to begin the games. This was an immensely proud moment for the entire family but Sura was shocked when she saw the look on Julia's face as she watched her father. Pure bitterness poured from her. Like heat, her anger seemed to almost ripple the air around her. Cornelius now raised his hand and in a clear, strong voice spoke. "Those who are about to fight, we salute you!"

The animal hunts, the venationes, were always first. After the parade the animals in the cages had been returned to pens beneath the arena. A net was immediately put up to protect those spectators who sat the closest. Cornelius Petreius gave a signal. Gates were raised, and half a dozen lions and several panthers stampeded into the arena to the cheers of the crowd. There was a deafening roar as an elephant lumbered out from another gated opening and stood for several seconds looking slightly dazed and confused. Then from the far side of the arena twenty venatores, trained hunters, ran out with their javelins hoisted.

"Bravo, brother! An elephant. That must have cost you!" Marcus's father said to Cornelius Petreius.

"Nothing is too good for Pompeii," Cornelius Petreius replied in a voice loud enough to be heard by anyone remotely close to where the family sat. A wave of applause rose from the surrounding spectators and a scatter of "Hail Petreius" could be heard.

Yet Julia seethed. Did no one else notice it? Sura wondered. Julia must have found out about the plan to send her to the Temple of Damia. She had arrived with Marcus. Had he actually told her? But he had made Sura swear not to say a word. Well, there was not time for this now, Sura thought. She must pray for her brother. Gavianus and Bryzos were the fourth pair scheduled to fight.

The minutes dragged on. It was agonizing. The first pair featured a secutor, or chaser, and a dimachaerus, a gladiator who fought with two swords. The technique was for the secutor to chase his opponent around the field exhausting him. The secutor wore full helmet with tiny eye-holes, which limited his vision considerably, and his two-sworded opponent, although not as fast a runner, had a strategy that seemed to be paying off. The opponent insisted, quite boldly, on fighting close. Not running, but rather dodging. The dimachaerus's footwork of shifts and dodges was magnificent.

"By Jupiter!" Cornelius Petreius exclaimed. "This fellow is wearing the secutor out with hardly any running at all."

A clash rang out and then there was a flash of something spinning through the air. It all happened quite suddenly. The secutor was down, his sword struck from his hand. Sprays of blood dappled the sunlight—for in fact the hand had taken flight with the sword.

The crowd roared their approval. "Oh, dear!" Cornelius turned to Flavia's husband, Cuspius Pansa. "Now what is our dear lanista Aurelius going to do with a one-handed gladiator?"

"One combat too many for this secutor, but he was good in his day. Faustinus will use him as a teacher," Cuspius Pansa replied.

Immediately handkerchiefs were raised and waved in the air and the cry to spare him went up. This was purely formal. It was very seldom that the gladiator was commanded to kill his opponent. The crowd knew that these fighters cost dearly and could not be merely thrown away. Over the years this secutor had pleased them. Cornelius Petreius stood up, his thumb raised high over his head giving the missum, the signal that the secutor's life should be spared. Sura saw Julia again looking at him intently, but not with bitterness. She looked as if she was about to cry. What was going on with her dear mistress?

Then time seemed to quicken for Sura. Before she knew it, the fourth pair of gladiators was standing in front of the podium offering their respects to the sponsor as was customary. Livia was standing up cheering madly. The sun gleamed off Gavianus's trident, and his net was draped almost casually over his shoulder. Bryzos carried a shield and his broad sword. That was all. It was a contest between the fishman and the fisherman, for that was what the murmillo and the retiarus were modeled on.

To Sura it seemed like an unfair match. The murmillo had no chance of getting close. He had to escape the periphery of the net when it was cast. His sword could not compare in length with the trident. In the past, Bryzos's skill had been in separating the retiarius from his net and thus throwing him off balance. Would it work this time?

Sura's fists were clenched in her lap. With every fiber of her body she willed her brother quickness and strength. The combat began with an agonizing intensity as the two gladiators started to circle each other. Gavianus coaxed Bryzos into making a few feinting thrusts. He wanted to judge the range of his opponent with his sword and to see how he manipulated his shield.

Then Bryzos made a bold dash close in. Gavianus threw the net, but Bryzos was out of range by the time it landed. *Good*, thought Sura, *now he knows how wide that net can be cast*.

This went on for some time. Sura could feel the crowd growing impatient. There were a few shouts. "Hurry up with it fishman!" But neither the fishman nor the fisherman were to be rushed.

Bryzos darted in once more. This time Gavianus did not throw the net. He had barely retreated when Bryzos immediately began another rush. Gavianus looked startled at the quickness, and this time threw the net. But it was a bad throw, and once more Bryzos escaped.

"He's thinking offensively, my dear. Quite unusual for a murmillo," Livia's husband Marcus leaned over and said to her. "Wouldn't you say this fellow has our Gavianus stumped? He's having to think defensively."

"No. Never," she said firmly. "It's a ruse."

Was it a ruse? Sura wondered frantically. *If so, did Bryzos see it?* There was a sudden tremendous roar from the crowd. The fisherman had thrown his net. It had not caught Bryzos but his sword. Once again Sura saw a blade go flying through the air. *By the gods he has nothing now*, she thought. *Only his shield.*

Livia clapped her hands gleefully. "You call that defensive, Marcus? I told you he was clever."

Sura wanted to put her hands around the woman's fat neck and strangle her. What would Bryzos do now? *Please, dear gods, help him. Help him. He has been caught once by a net. Not again.* Julia turned around and looked at Sura. But Sura merely shook her head.

Bryzos appeared very cool, despite his vulnerable state. With an almost casual air he began walking around in a lazy circle. The crowd began to boo. This was terrible. If they were booing now, if Bryzos was wounded they would demand a kill and not mercy. Gavianus was between Bryzos and his sword. To get to it Bryzos would have to come within range of the net. It was an impossible situation.

Gavianus could rush him at any second and cast his net, and Bryzos would have absolutely nothing with which to protect himself. His only hope would be to separate Gavianus from his net, but Gavianus would still have the trident and Bryzos would have nothing. Bryzos was moving more quickly now but he was nowhere near his sword. Still he was definitely making Gavianus move about. First he was here, and then there. He was living up to his name, Bryzos, which meant "quick" in the Thracian language.

"What's the fellow doing?" Sura heard someone say. A hush had fallen upon the spectators. The sun beat down on the arena. The shadows that minutes ago had seemed short had lengthened imperceptibly. It was when Sura saw the two shadows, the one of her brother and that of Gavianus briefly intersect, that it burst upon her what Bryzos's strategy was. He had maneuvered Gavianus so that he was facing east, but Bryzos was facing west into the setting sun. Bryzos now began manipulating his shield. His only defense had now become his offense. He was using the shield as a weapon. The sun began flashing off it, and blades of light cut through the air. The retiarius wore no helmet, thus no visor. From where Sura sat she could see Gavianus hesitate. *Bryzos is blinding him!*

Sura began to hear whispers:

"What's wrong with Gavianus?"

"The clever fellow is blinding him. Look at the sun bouncing off his shield."

"The net's cumbersome. Why not drop it for a moment and get out of the glare?"

"Drop his net? You show me a retiarius who would willingly drop his net. Gavianus is no fool. He's biding his time and holding his position. As soon as the sun drops behind the walls of the amphitheater there won't be any problem for him. He's just waiting."

The hairs on the back of Sura's neck stood up. The man was right. Oh, if only she could stay the sun in its course. *Apollo! God of the sun, stop the sun*, Sura closed her eyes and prayed. But when she opened them again, the sun was on its inexorable course. In another minute, or perhaps just a few seconds, it would be behind the walls of the amphitheater.

It was not even a minute, and Gavianus wasted not a second. He rushed at Bryzos and flung the net. Bryzos dodged to the side, and there was the sound of the net clanging against the shield, but he was not caught. Gavianus was furious and wheeled about. At just that moment there was a crash of thunder. Lightning streaked down over the top of Vesuvius, illuminating the mountain in an eerie glow. Bryzos tilted his shield. There was a second flash as the shield reflected the bolt. Gavianus stumbled slightly, then rushed forward and hurled his trident. The crowd was on its feet. "It hit him! It hit him!" There was a shrill scream.

Sura could not see. She climbed atop her seat. Blood coursed down her brother's arm. The entire arm hung at an odd angle. Gavianus had been separated from his net. His trident lay at Bryzos's feet. Bryzos bent down and picked up the trident. Despite the fact that both men were separated from their weapons, it was obvious who the winner was—the one who had used the weapons of the gods: sun and thunder. The crowd was crying Bryzos's name.

Gavianus looked as if he were in shock. Livia sank down in her seat and buried her face in her hands.

"Vulcan's hero!" someone shouted.

Cornelius Petreius stood up and signaled that the combat was finished. Both fighters were summoned to stand in front of the podium. Bryzos's arm was bleeding badly. Cornelius Petreius presented him with the palm of victory and he walked shakily from the arena.

Sura got up and rushed out. She immediately went to the corridor beneath the arena where there was a bay for wounded gladiators. By the time she reached her brother, he lay on a stretcher unconscious. A doctor was bending over him.

"You should not be here," someone said.

"I'm his sister."

"No matter, get out."

"Let her stay," said the doctor.

"Will he be all right? Will he get better?" Sura was frantic. Her eyes scoured the doctor's face for a sign of hope.

"Get better? Perhaps. Fight again? Never. His arm is ruined, and he has lost a lot of blood."

The bloodstained victory palm lay on Bryzos's chest. Sura came up to him. "Bryzos, it's me, Sura. You were magnificent." A pulse flickered beneath his eyes. They opened slowly.

"I'll never get caught in a net again, Sura, I swear."

"No you won't—ever."

"You take the palm."

"It's not mine. I didn't win."

"No matter. I have many. They bring luck. You take this one."

"Yes," she whispered, and let her lips brush his cheek, which was already feverish.

"Go now," the doctor said. "He's weak. You can come visit him tomorrow."

"Yes, yes, of course," Sura replied. She stood there for a moment wondering where to go. She did not want to return to the podium. She could not face Livia. It was best that she just go home. There was still much to do for the wedding tomorrow. Perhaps it would be better now to keep busy.

But Sura did not go directly home. She walked past the villa Petreius and straight on through the Forensa Gate to the Temple of Vulcan. The temple was deserted now, and in the gathering purple of the twilight she mounted the steps to the altar where the coals still smoldered. On the black stone a scene was carved that showed Vulcan as Quietus the allayer of fire, and Mulciber the charmer of fire.

"I have nothing to really to offer except my thanks. Had

I the money I would have brought a fish. Praised be Vulcan in all your names. In the name of Vulcan the all-powerful god of fire, in the name of Quietus the allayer of fire, and in the name of Mulciber, who charmed the fire from the sky, I offer you the only thing I have that I can call my own." She knelt down and lay the palm on the smoldering embers.

Sixteen

 JULIA STOOD IN CORNELIA'S ROOM. They had just finished the ceremony in which Cornelia had dedicated her toys, her clothes, and even her bulla to the household gods. Now her mother and a slave tucked Cornelia's hair, just washed and combed, into the crimson net for sleeping so it would not tangle and cause problems for the ornatrices in the morning hours, near dawn, before the wedding.

"I can't believe that it was just over a month ago that I was doing the same for Flavia on the eve of her wedding!" Herminia exclaimed.

"And now it is my turn!" Cornelia said, with more than a tinge of triumph in her voice.

And though I, too, shall marry, Julia thought as she watched this custom, *I shall never wear the crimson net.* She wondered where she might be on the night of her wedding. Marcus said they would go first to Rome and then perhaps farther north.

Herminia turned to her other daughter. "Julia, you seem quiet tonight, and during the games as well. Are you not feeling well? We can't have one of our bridesmaids ill."

"No, Mother, I am fine. Just a little tired."

"Well, you should go to bed early then."

"But do you know what you are supposed to do, Julia?" Cornelia snapped.

"Yes, Cornelia I have seen it done many times. After the sacrifice and after the witnessing of the contract, I watch Valeria lead you to Cassius's side and you join hands."

"Yes, and there will be no more of that bit of silliness like this morning at the Temple of Vulcan. No slipping of sleeves."

"Now, now, Cornelia," Herminia cautioned. "We have been through that already. It was an accident." Both Julia and Cornelia knew it was no such thing.

"But do you know what you are to do after the banquet, in the procession to my new home?" Cornelia asked.

"You have told me a dozen times, and if you recall I was in the procession when Flavia went to Cuspius's house. So I do know."

"But you were not a bridesmaid. It's different. For example, first are the torch bearers, and then the flute players, and Valeria will be right behind them, and then Flavia, and then you."

"I know. Valeria carries the distaff and Flavia carries the spindle and then when we arrive at the house and Cassius has carried you over the threshold Valeria will lead you to the couch." It would be Valeria's job to deliver the nova nupta, the newly married woman, to her bridegroom.

Of course Julia would not be there for it, because she and Marcus would have left at the height of the banquet when the guests were reeling with wine. *Too bad, Cornelia, you'll have to find someone else. Maybe Sura. Then you can wipe your dirty hands on her hair one last time.*

But every time Julia thought of Sura, something clenched deep inside her. It was wonderful that her brother had survived, had won. But he looked as if he had been badly wounded. What if Bryzos did die, and she herself had run off with Marcus? Poor Sura. She would be left with no one, except of course, the disgusting fuller Stephanus. She would be so alone. The thought of this was unbearable.

Julia came to her room, where Sura was waiting for her. She sat down at her dressing table. Sura began to take the pins from her hair and comb it. How many nights had they gone through this ritual? How accustomed she had grown to the feeling of Sura's fingertips working through her hair, gently untangling snarls, sweeping into submission a recalcitrant curl that sprung from a braid or a bun. She should pay attention, for how would she know how to do this by herself? She had barely even run a comb through her own hair. In a certain way it seemed like such a silly concern. But at the same time, it was symbolic to Julia of the change that was about to transpire and alter her and Sura's lives forever.

"So will your brother be all right, Sura?"

"I don't know. He has lost so much blood."

They continued talking for a few minutes. It was awkward and stiff for both of them. *She doesn't know that I know what she knows,* Julia thought. *Would she be surprised if I told her that I knew that I was to be given to the Temple of the Bona Dea, or that she had talked to Marcus, or that I know she is to be sold to Stephanus?* It suddenly seemed so ridiculous to Julia. This was the person that she was closest to in the world. She had never spent a night in her life without Sura sleeping on the pallet by her bed. And now what they were not saying lay like an immense ocean between them.

Julia raised her hand to the top of her head. She placed it on Sura's hand that was holding the comb. "Stop," she said.

"What?"

Julia turned around. She did not want this to be a mirror conversation.

"Sura, I know."

Sura's lower lip began to tremble. "You know what, Julia?"

"I know everything. Marcus told me."

"You know about the Temple of Damia?"

"Yes, and I know about your being sold to Stephanus." Sura dropped her head.

"Do you want to run away, Sura?"

A shudder seemed to pass through Sura. She tried to speak but nothing came out. Then she looked at Julia. "I wanted to. But my brother said I should not. It would be worse if I was caught. He said that soon he will have earned enough money to buy his freedom, and mine."

"Do you think that's true?"

She shrugged. "I think he wants it to be true. However, the doctor says he shall never fight again. So I do not think this will come to pass. But what about you?"

"It seems that we are both slaves," Julia said with a wry smile.

"Yes, it would seem that way."

"Well," said Julia softly, "I plan to run away."

"You what?" Sura's eyes sparkled.

"Marcus and I shall run away together and get married."

"But he's promised to Drusilla."

"And I am promised to the Temple of Damia."

"You shall both be disowned."

"I have already been disowned by my parents." A hard light glinted in Julia's eyes. It was the same light, the same expression that had so startled Sura when she had seen Julia looking at her father at the games. "What does it matter if you are disowned if you have never owned yourself to begin with?"

Sura fell to her knees and embraced Julia. Julia stroked her head. "Julia, you were like my baby, my baby doll when I came here. My poppet, and now, though I am four years older than you, I feel that you are older than I am."

"I feel old," Julia said. "So old."

"I shall miss you so."

"I would take you. But then that would make me a thief."

"No, I'll be all right. Don't worry."

"There is no way I won't worry."

"Try not to. My brother is here." There was a quaver in Sura's voice. "Tell me, Julia, how do you plan this escape? When will it happen?"

"It will happen midway through Cornelia's wedding banquet when all the guests are very drunk," she whispered. She continued to tell Sura other details of their plan for escape.

"I shall help you, Julia. If I cannot have freedom for myself I shall borrow the joy of it from you!" There was sheer delight in her eyes.

Julia leaned back, lifted her lame arm, and put it atop Sura's shoulder and then placed her other hand on her other shoulder. "You are not, nor have you ever been, my slave. You are my sister."

Seventeen

HERMINIA WAS KNEELING ON THE floor as she tied the woolen band around the waist of Cornelia's tunic.

"With joy and with honor I tie this girdle and make the knot of Hercules, the guardian of married life." She rose and gave her daughter a kiss on each cheek.

For Julia it seemed that no time had passed between when she had stood watching her mother fix Cornelia's hair the previous evening and now just past dawn. For here she was again in her mother's dressing room. The ornatrices, Cornelia's slave, her mother's slave, Valeria, and now Flavia with her slave were all in attendance as the bride was being dressed. There was much giggling and excitement. Somehow despite all the laughing and talk, Julia realized it had been strangely quiet all morning. She had not yet heard the song of one bird. This was peculiar. There was always birdsong in the garden from the first light of the new day, or even before.

"Julia!" her mother was saying in a loud voice. "Are you dreaming?"

"What?"

"The hairdresser wants to adjust the ribbons in your hair."

"Oh yes, of course," she said lightly, and smiled. "They are rather crooked now, aren't they?"

Julia tried to join in to the festive spirit of the morning as best she could. She was no actress but she must try. Yesterday had been perhaps the most unbelievable day of her life. And yet she had barely had time to think about Marcus telling her that he loved her. That he wanted only her. It seemed miraculous. She had never expected to marry at all. She realized that there had never been anyone in her life like Marcus, and now it made perfect sense that they would spend the rest of their lives together. Yesterday she had been too stunned to be truly excited. But today she was, and this made the acting a bit easier. It was even easy to be nice to Cornelia.

Julia looked at her older sister. "You look beautiful, Cornelia," she said, and she really did mean it. Cornelia looked absolutely magnificent in the traditional woven tunic made in the ancient way from one piece of fabric, tied at the waist with the marriage knot of Hercules, and then falling straight to the floor. Over this tunic she wore a saffron-colored palla, with sandals of a matching color. Her bulla had been exchanged for a silver collar.

Her beautiful nearly white blonde hair had been dressed in the traditional style of the Vestal Virgins, which was the way all brides wore their hair on their wedding day. It was a complicated procedure for which she had to rise before dawn. Two ornatrices had worked together, one on each side of her. They first divided her hair into six locks. These were arranged over pads of artificial hair. It was then all tied in place by ribbons and over this Cornelia wore the flammeum, a veil of flaming orange that covered her forehead. Atop the veil a wreath had been pinned woven from myrtle and orange blossom. The entire house had been festooned in garlands of orange blossoms, myrtle, verbena, and sweet marjoram. Doorways were swagged with ribbons and more blossoms. It looked as it were a house for the gods with the profusion of flowers.

Dressing the bride had taken almost five hours. It was almost time for them to go down to the atrium to greet the guests.

"Wait!" Cornelia said suddenly. She and her mother looked at Julia and exchanged tiny excited smiles. Julia felt a new dread well up in her. Cornelia turned to a slave and nodded. The slave scurried out of the room. A minute later she was back carrying a birdcage. In it was a spectacular parrot with feathers the colors of sapphires and emeralds. Julia gasped as Cornelia took the cage from the slave and brought it to her.

"For you, Julia. It is the custom that the bride give each bridesmaid a gift. I have already given Flavia and Valeria their presents."

"Cornelia! It's the same one—the one from the market."

"Not the very same, but close, I think."

"Cornelia, I . . . don't know what to say." Julia leaned forward to kiss her sister. Just as her lips brushed her sister's cheeks she saw the tears brimming in her mother's eyes and it struck her. *This is not just the gift for a bridesmaid, this is my good-bye gift. Something for me to take to the Temple of Damia!* She looked at the bird in all its splendor and suddenly hated it. *Pretend, Julia! Pretend. Be strong!* She squeezed her eyes shut for a brief instant, cleared her throat, and spoke. "This is so kind of you. I'm sure that he—is it a he?"

"We think so," Cornelia giggled.

"I'm sure he and I shall become great friends." Julia pulled her mouth into a harsh bright smile.

"Now we must hurry along, girls. The guests will be arriving." Herminia began to walk from the room. Julia turned to Sura and handed her the cage. "We must think of a name for the dear creature. Take him to my room."

Julia, Cornelia, and Flavia followed their mother to the first atrium where their father and Tiberius Calpurnius

Maius, the auspex, were waiting for them. It was by this time after noon. The first guests to arrive were Marcus and his family.

"You look splendid, Marcus!" Cornelius Petreius exclaimed as they entered the atrium. Julia and Marcus exchanged a quick nervous glance. Marcus looked extremely handsome in his new toga. He seemed taller, bigger to Julia. He seemed a man. *But am I really yet a woman?* she wondered.

Cassius and his family came through door. *None of this will be happening for me,* Julia thought. *There will be no flowers, no auspex. Nothing. My marriage to Marcus will be the marriage of plebeians.*

With the wedding party assembled and the auspex leading the way, the family proceeded into the second atrium for the sacrifice to the gods and the drawing up of the marriage contract. The witnesses, Quintilius Pomponius and some of her father's other associates along with those of the groom's family, affixed their seals silently to the documents.

Two slaves stood at the side of the atrium holding a pig. Everyone took a step back as the auspex drew out a knife. There were stories about brides and guests being splattered by spurting blood. Julia just hoped that the palsied old auspex would not make a mess of things and fail to kill the pig cleanly. She envisioned the animal running wild, spurting blood all over the atrium. The blade glinted in a shaft of sunlight, and then without as much as a squeal, the pig simply plopped dead on the floor.

A slave quickly put an urn under the animal's slit neck to collect the blood, and placed it on a table next to the cup of nuptial wine. The auspex then proceeded with his business and sliced open the pig's belly to extract the entrails. He bent over the steaming coils of intestines. This was perhaps the tensest moment of the entire wedding. If, after examination, the entrails were deemed unfavorable the wedding was instantly canceled. This examination did not happen within a single moment but over several minutes. Poking at the entrails with a rod, the auspex seemed completely absorbed. Sometimes he would probe a bit deeper then lift one dripping portion to smell it. He would squint, then look again. It seemed to take forever, longer than it had at Flavia's wedding. But as soon as the auspex dropped the last of the intestines back onto the steaming bloody mass he smiled, and Julia knew that he was about to lie. It was almost the same smile the haruspex had worn that day when he read the entrails of the chicken and then proceeded to say that the omens were good for this date.

"All hear my conclusion, with the gods as my witness, the auspices are favorable. The marriage ceremony may proceed."

There was a collective sigh of relief. As soon as the

slaves had cleaned up the blood and mess of the sacrifice, the auspex nodded at Julia and she took her sister's hand and led her to Cassius's side. They stood in front of the table with the bowl of the pig's blood and the cup of wine

"Ubi tu Cassius, ego Cassia. Where you are Cassius, I am the wife of Cassius."

But, thought Julia, *where will* we *be? Where will Marcus and I be?*

Eighteen

AS CORNELIA AND CASSIUS UTTERED the final words of their marriage vow, Julia felt a vibration come up through the floor of the atrium. This was followed by a rattle, and she watched transfixed as the bowl of blood and the wine began to tremble then jitter across the table in a peculiar little dance. She looked in amazement at this odd spectacle. *The bowl and cup are actually going to fall off the table!* Seconds later there was a crash.

Cornelia yelped.

"What's happening?" her mother cried out. And then there was an enormous boom. Beneath them the tile floor began to split open.

"Quick, into the garden! That will be the safest place," Cornelius ordered.

Marcus was grabbing her hand. "Is it an earthquake?" Julia asked.

"I don't think so," he answered. "Can't you smell it?"

Marcus was right, there was something different in the air. "It's like the smell of the fountain that night," Julia gasped.

"Rotten eggs. Sulfur from deep inside the earth. No wonder the fountains were running dry—the earth was cracking from within and the aqueducts were shattering."

"So it *is* an earthquake?"

The color had drained from Marcus's face. "I think worse."

"My wedding! It's ruined!" Cornelia wailed. Julia turned to look at her sister. The flaming orange veil she wore was sprinkled with white, and as she looked up it appeared to be snowing.

Julia held her hand, and the flakes fell gently on it. It was not snow. These pieces were warm, some like large lumps of sand. "What in the world?" she whispered. Something scratched at the back of Julia's brain as she stared transfixed by the bits that were collecting around her sandals. Already they were up to her toes. She looked at Cornelia, whose veil now was almost completely white.

"It's ash and stone, pumice!" Marcus said, his voice taut. "Come with me, Julia." He took her by the hand.

"Where are we going?"

"Where is there a high window facing out?"

"My room, actually."

There was so much confusion that no one noticed them leave.

As soon as they entered the room, Marcus threw open the shutters. Gusts of hot air blasted into the room. The parrot was squawking madly and bashing its wings against the sides of its cage.

"By the gods!" he exclaimed. "Look, Julia!" Outside it was a blizzard of ash and pumice. "Look at Vesuvius . . . Vulcan's fist!" What had once been a summit had vanished under an enormous roiling billow of smoke. They watched mesmerized as a cloud that was the shape of an umbrella pine tree with a thick trunk began to grow out of the mountain itself.

Indeed it looked exactly as if a fist had punched through the summit of Vesuvius. It was no longer a summit but a gaping mouth belching smoke, vomiting flames. The flames appeared weirdly bright behind the scrim of snowflakes. *Take care, my dear, and remember as hot as it is now, when snow comes in summer that is the time to leave.*

The words of the Sibyl of Sarnus rushed through Julia's mind like gusts of wind.

"We must go now!" Julia screamed. "Now, Marcus. It was the prophecy of the sibyl."

Marcus looked confused. Julia knew that there was no time to explain about the Sybil of Sarnus. "We have to go!"

"You are right," Marcus whispered. "Now is the perfect time." They looked down. The streets were pandemonium as people rushed toward the gates of the city. "Just wait for one second. I have to go back down. I have something. I must get my pouch."

"Leave it!" Julia cried.

"No, it's too important!"

He raced out of the room, almost bumping into Sura, who was coming in.

"Sura!" They ran into each other's arms. "Sura, you must come with us. It is the perfect time."

"But my brother?"

"The barracks are all the way across the city. We must leave from here, close to the gates."

"But he is too sick to leave. I can't abandon him."

"Sura, be reasonable. There are dozens of gladiators who can help him. He won't be abandoned. But you shall be abandoning your only chance for freedom. It is your life."

"I have to think." Sura's eyes darted as if seeking an answer, a sign as to what she must do.

"There is not time to think," Julia said. She realized that it should not have taken this long for Marcus to come back. "Where is Marcus?" she cried desperately. It suddenly seemed to grow darker in the room. Sura ran to the window. "A huge cloud, Julia!"

Julia looked out. An immense black cloud was rolling toward Pompeii. It was as if the shutters of the sky were being closed. Thunder shook the air, and suddenly it was dusk. The white pumice had turned to gray. Bigger stones were now falling. The day had vanished into a sudden night laced with missiles hurling through the dark. Julia saw a large man knocked over in the street below. He did not get up.

"Where is he? Where is Marcus?" Julia screamed, and rushed out of her bedroom. Standing on the balcony, she looked down into the garden, which was now white. The spaces that had once been green were completely covered. The pool floated with white chunks as if pieces of clouds had fallen from the sky onto the water. The statue of the reclining Venus was buried almost to her neck.

"Where is everybody? Sura! There is no one in the garden."

"They are probably inside to protect themselves."

"But where is Marcus?"

"I don't know. I saw his mother flee from the villa just before I came up to you."

"Aunt Livia left?"

"Yes. I was tempted to go with her."

"Why?"

"She was going to the gladiator barracks I am sure."

At just that moment the whole house shook and there was a crash.

"The roof of the atrium!" Sura cried.

"By the gods that is where Marcus was going!"

Sura grabbed her. "Julia, don't go down there." In the next moment they heard a thunderous crash as a roof in another part of the house collapsed.

The terror, the confusion had left Sura's eyes. "Julia, we must go now if we are to live! We can crawl out your bedroom window before that roof goes."

"But Marcus?"

"Julia, somehow he will find us. You told me minutes ago not to abandon my only chance for freedom. It is exactly as you said—there *is* no time to think. Come now. Marcus and Bryzos will find us."

"Wait! The bird." Julia rushed over to the parrot and opened the cage door. "Fly out!" she shouted at it. But the parrot still continued bashing its wings against the slats of the cage.

"It doesn't know it's free!" Sura's voice was tight.

"Fly, you fool!" Julia commanded. She tipped the cage over and the bird fell out, tumbling to the floor. It appeared stunned.

"It's wings have been clipped. It probably can't fly," Sura said. Then she took Julia by the shoulders and shook her. "But we can. We have to go *now*!"

In a daze Julia allowed herself to be led to the window by Sura.

Nineteen

THEY LOWERED THEMSELVES FROM the window down the sloping roof, and it was just a short drop from the roof's edge to the streets piled high with ash and pumice. People coated with ash appeared as lumbering statues. They could no longer run, so they climbed thickly through the fallen debris. A man's face loomed in front of them like a death mask. The two girls joined a flow of people going through the Forensa Gate. They each covered their mouths with one hand. Before they left they had grabbed pillows, and now held them over their heads to protect themselves from the falling rock.

But where, Julia thought, *does one go when the world begins to tear apart, when the day turns to night and the sky reels with burning rocks and cinders? Where does one hide?*

"It's not like snow anymore," Julia said.

"What are you talking about?" Sura asked. Her question seemed to break through Julia's confusion.

"We have to go to the mouth of the Sarnus. We must see the sibyl. She is the one!" Julia said.

"The one what?"

"She predicted all of this. She said that it would snow in summer, and look, the falling ash and stone looks like snow but . . ." She didn't finish the thought. "Come, there is no time to waste. We should go by way of the Stabian Gate to the Sarnus. That will be closest. We must hurry."

They hurried as best they could through the procession of ghosts and death masks. Even animals, dogs, cats, donkeys had turned white. Ahead of them an ox foundered and dropped to its knees. It bellowed as it tried rise from the debris. A few steps beyond the ox a chained dog's eyes rolled back in terror as it began to die in a tangled agony. At the corner of the Via dell'Abbondanza and a smaller street by the shop of Stephanus the fuller, they turned right to follow a road to the gate. Through the open front of the shop they could see stunned workers and Stephanus himself clutching a bag and yelling.

"Thieves, you're all thieves!" He crushed the bag to his chest.

The two girls rushed on by. Julia stole one look back at Vesuvius. From its mouth an immense fountain of rock and ash blasted even higher than before into darkness.

Shrill cries rang out into the night spinning with cinders. The girls passed familiar shops that had been transformed by the blizzard of ash and pumice. The groaning and frantic yelps of trapped animals mixed with the cries of children and babies. But Julia and Sura continued to plow their way through the hail of ash and rock. Lightning and flames fractured the darkness, and Julia nearly laughed as she saw a woman standing stock still up to her waist in ash and clucking madly at the bolts of lightning. Yet another superstition of how to ward off Vulcan! It now seemed completely ridiculous to her. This was beyond a god's displeasure, beyond his anger. This was the earth committing suicide.

A maniacal, mindless mob rushed through the gates. People pushed and shoved. An old lady fell and was trampled. A mother screamed as she dropped her baby and then lay down beside it to die. Julia and Sura clung to each other and were borne by the momentum of this tide as they desperately tried to keep each other afloat. There was one moment when Sura floundered, but through some torrent of sudden energy, Julia wrenched her clear of the debris and stampede of feet.

How they ever survived the surge through the gates Julia did not know but when they reached the port they encountered a strange sight. The sea had begun to retreat drastically. And where there was still water, the harbor was clogged with floating pieces of rock. Every boat was locked in, their hulls scraping noisily against the floating rocks. It was a low, painful creaking and moaning as if boats were protesting their stone prison. Several boats appeared half sunk from the load of rocks on their decks.

The girls followed the port road. Flames tore at the night like scimitars. And as Julia looked back through the hail of falling rock she saw gaping wounds on the flanks of Vesuvius. It reminded her of the pig that had been sacrificed hours ago. The earth's entrails spilled from the mountainside, writhing and bulging as if still pumping blood. As they walked, lightning bolts wove the night into an electric cloth of eerie brightness. The air was shaking with unceasing thunder now. But on the edge of this sound there was a peculiar hissing murmur. It threaded through the clamor of the thunder, and a noxious smell began to fill the air. Julia looked back. Flames were advancing toward the city. For one instant she was tempted to turn around, to flee back—to Marcus, to the only love she would know, could know. Marcus, her only hope. Ubi tu Marcus ego Marcia. The words rang in her head, battered her brain. *I never got to make the most sacred of vows.* She wheeled about. Sura was horrified. She grabbed her by the shoulders.

"Where are you going?"

"I have to go back for Marcus."

Sura's eyes opened wide. A green fiery glint sprung from

them. She raised her hand and slapped Julia's face, hard. "I did not go back for my brother. You will not got back for Marcus. Look, we are almost to the mouth of the river."

Indeed they were. And there was water! Not a lot but some flowed from the river to meet the retreating sea. *Even the sea is fleeing,* Julia thought, *even the sea!*

Twenty

 JULIA STOOD AT THE OPENING of the cave. For the first time the shadows were welcoming. They almost seemed to beckon her. She took Sura's hand and together they stepped inside. Julia squinted into the gray light of the cave. It felt safe and cool and at last they were free from the constant bombardment of ash and pumice.

"You have come." The melting voice from far back in the cave drifted toward them. Julia's chest tightened and she squeezed Sura's hand. She heard light footsteps. The shadows dissolved. A familiar figure stood in front of them.

Julia gasped. "Mother!"

"No, dear. I am your aunt, your mother's twin. My name is Aurelia." She raised her right hand in greeting. Her left arm hung limp and withered by her side.

Julia tilted her head in stunned disbelief. "I . . . I . . ." she hesitated. "Don't understand."

"I know dear, I know."

"But I never knew my mother had a sister."

"No one in Pompeii knew, not even your father, not for a very long time. In those days such things were a dark secret. And even today, as I am sure you are aware, females with deformities, well, I needn't tell you. I think you know."

"But why didn't Mother tell me that there was someone like me? I would have felt better."

"I am sure your parents would have told you eventually, but they were fearful, for several reasons. People prefer to think of sibyls as being without families, or at least families nearby and known. Somehow that an ordinary family would have a seer or a sibyl almost seems to diminish the power of that person's prophecy. Secondly, I imagine that they were afraid that if you knew too young you might let it slip sometime to a friend or family member. Since your grandparents died, only your mother and father knew. You have to remember, Julia, that your father had ambitions. He is a successful businessman and now a magistrate and a member of the ordo."

"What you are saying is that it could have destroyed his career," Julia replied bitterly.

"Julia, it is not as if you have not benefited from your father's success." She paused and turned toward Sura. "And who is this young woman?"

"Oh, this is Sura, my slave, no, I don't think she is my slave anymore." She glanced first at Sura then at her aunt.

"Nothing is really the same as it was." She hesitated, then turned and looked out the cave opening toward Vesuvius. "What has happened? I thought it was just a mountain."

"We all did," her aunt replied. "But it was a volcano."

Julia squeezed her eyes shut. She was a welter of confusing emotions. One second she was trying to comprehend how a mountain had turned into a roaring fiery beast, and the next how her parents had hidden the secret of her aunt, the Sibyl of Sarnus, from her for so long. It crossed her mind suddenly that perhaps her own withered arm was not the Curse of Venus but a curse of a different sort—punishment to a family for hiding away another human being, denying the existence of Aurelia—daughter, aunt, sister. And now they had been ready to do the same thing again—hide Julia, not in a cave but in the Temple of Damia.

"They were going to hide me away just as you have been hidden," Julia blurted out.

"What? What are you saying?" The sibyl leaned closer to her. It was so strange seeing this face that was identical to her mother's but not her mother.

"They had planned to send me to that awful place," Julia whispered hoarsely.

"What awful place?"

"The Temple of Damia."

Aurelia shut her eyes. Her breath caught in her throat. Her voice sounded raw when she spoke now. "I was fearful of this. So they were really going to do it." Julia was not sure if it was a question or a statement, but once more she felt a bitterness like bile rising within her.

"Yes, they were really going to do it!" She looked sharply at her aunt now. "Why didn't they send you to the temple when you were younger?"

"Well, for one thing, the Temple of Damia was not yet as widespread. It was just one more new religion imported from the east. It had no status. But most important, it was my mother, your grandmother, who sensed that I had second sight. When I turned six I was taken to a seer far from here. And then when I grew older I came here."

"Why here?"

"I know the river. I read the river."

"Not fish eyes? You don't read fish's eyeballs?"

The sybil laughed. "No, not ever. That is just an old tale. It was the river that told me that something like this might happen. Odd things were occurring. Being a seer is not about seeing into the future but being aware of the present and the changes." It was almost too much for Julia to take in.

"You have lived alone all these years? Studying the river?"

"All alone. But your mother would come to visit me often."

"It's so sad."

"It was the way it was. I was lucky not to be put out for the wolves."

"Your father would have done that?"

"No, but he kept me hidden away. Only one slave was ever allowed to attend to me. I was never permitted to go into town and I could only go into the garden late at night."

"After you went away didn't you miss your mother, or my mother, your sister?"

"Oh yes, yes indeed. But—" she hesitated. "When I lived with the seer of Sullum, I could live free. I roamed the hills of the countryside. I felt the wind. I grew brown in the sun and at night I felt the tingle of the stars in the sky."

"Are you really a seer?"

At this Aurelia smiled wryly. "When the snow fell in summer, you came, didn't you?"

Julia nodded her head. "It's true." She paused. "But what else did you see? Did you see my parents? Marcus? Are they . . . are they . . . ?" her voice caught.

"Marcus?" Aurelia asked.

Tears began leaking from Julia's eyes. Sura came close and put her arm around her shoulders. "Marcus was her cousin. They were in love. They planned to run away and marry."

"I saw none of that. I do not know if your parents will live or die, but I did—how should I explain it? I saw, or I felt deep within me, that you might live through this."

"But how did you know what *this* was, what was going to happen? How did you know about this terrible . . . ?"

And once more she turned toward Vesuvius in disbelief. "It was just a mountain with green slopes and vineyards and . . ." Her voice trailed off.

"I live in a cave. I live close to the earth. I hear its sighs. I feel its odd twitches. I sense the changes in the temperatures of the river that runs its course down from the hills. I know its queer scents. The smell of dust and rock. I feel the variations of its deepest writhings and stirrings of its entrails. The disharmonies, the rhythms. The day you came with your mother almost a month ago the bats left. That morning, in the broad light of day, they began to drop like flakes of rock, like tiles from a ceiling. I knew . . . I knew . . . Venus is your mother's goddess, but mine is Gaia, the earth's mother. She is my goddess and my mother. She taught me well and I learned her ways."

As her aunt spoke Julia began to realize that Aurelia was not talking nonsense. Her vision had nothing to do with "prophetic chickens," or pigs. Her insights came from being an attentive listener to the earth's ways. Her vision was informed by knowledge and not superstition. *How Marcus would have loved this explanation*, she thought. But at that moment, Julia sensed that she had lost Marcus forever. She took Sura's hand and held it tightly.

"Aunt Aurelia, where should we go?'

"We shall walk away until we meet the sea. The river and us, we all seek the same thing—the sea."

Julia and Sura looked in the direction Aurelia was

now gazing. They could just make out the shape of sails on the horizon. *I've seen this before,* Julia thought suddenly, and then remembered the baths and how three weeks before she had tipped her head against the edge of the pool and imagined herself on one of the painted boats, sailing straight out across the bay to a distant horizon, away on a boundless blue sea.

"Yes, away," she whispered. "Away."

Through a screen of falling ash, three figures could be seen wading toward the sea, where boats bobbed against the sky. Julia and Sura, holding hands, turned back one last time. They looked at their city through scrims of tears. Time had stopped for Pompeii, but for two young girls it was just beginning.

Epilogue

IN THE VILLA OF CORNELIUS Petreius, only one body was found, that of Marcus Cornelius Drusus. He clutched in his fist a pouch that contained a wedding band. At the corner of Via dell'Abbondanza, the body of Stephanus the fuller was uncovered still grasping a key in one hand and a bag of gold coins in another. Just outside the Stabian Gate, a group of people were found that included a young woman whose hair had been divided into six locks and arranged over pads of artificial hair in the traditional style of brides on their wedding day. It was Cornelia. And atop her head, inscribed in ash, was a wreath of myrtle and orange blossom. Embracing the bride was her husband, Cassius.

A few feet away was Herminia Petreia. Her husband, who had fallen near her, was trying to protect her head with a pillow. Her fingers had been cemented to an amber pendant of Cupid that hung around her neck. Cornelius's brother Marcus lay next to him, and nearby Flavia had fallen facedown with a piece of woven cloth over her mouth. The family group had fled from the villa of Petreius on Via di Mercurio and had barely time to escape the house before the gusting winds of poisonous gas overtook them.

And in the gladiators' barracks, the jewel-encrusted body of Livia Octavia was found in the chamber of one of the gladiators.

Julia and Sura knew none of this. They soon began a new life in the hill country far from Pompeii with the Sibyl of Sarnus, Julia's aunt Aurelia. They did not live in a cave as sibyl, slave, and mistress, but in a small farm villa as grape growers where, with Aurelia's guidance, they coaxed life from a south-facing slope. They tried not to think of the city they had left behind in ashes and the people they had loved. Julia and Sura had no way of finding out exactly who had been spared from Vesuvius's murderous eruption. To them, it was as if they were the last girls of Pompeii, and the first to build a new life after the death of their city.

Author's Note

"IT'S LIKE A CITY FROZEN IN TIME." My older sister's description was the first time I had ever heard of Pompeii, and I was instantly fascinated. I was perhaps in the second or third grade. I went to the *World Book Encyclopedia* and looked it up. Then I went to the library and found as many books as I could, but there were not all that many, at least not ones that I could read. There was, of course, no Internet in those days. But what I did read amazed me. I could not quite grasp that life had been brought to such a complete standstill within a period of about twenty-five hours. But perhaps the most intriguing fact was that this city had lain buried, a secret, for over fifteen hundred years.

I would not visit Pompeii for the first time until the spring of 2005, after I had decided to write this book. I really had to see it for myself. Going to Pompeii helped me create the family of Julia Petreia, which is completely fictional but is based on much research.

When I visited Pompeii it seemed like a city that was poised in a delicate state of suspension, a city waiting to have life breathed into it. I walked the streets for hours photographing the architecture and the remnants of the gardens, and studying the casts.

I took a great deal of time when I was visiting Pompeii to find the perfect house for the family of Julia Petreia. The street was easy—the Via di Mercurio in one of the wealthy sections of town. But there were too many perfect houses, and I had to be careful, for some of them—such as the House of the Faun with its beautiful sculpted faun shading an indoor pool and brilliant mosaic showing the battle between Alexander the Great and Darius III—are too famous for a fictional family to live in. I decided to take an atrium of one house, a garden of another, a street that I thought was the right one for my family, and put them all together. My husband, an architect, made me a drawing of a house for my fictional family right down to the yard for raising dormice (and yes, dormice were a favorite food of ancient Romans).

Speaking of food, I found it odd that the Roman culture of this time knew nothing of tomatoes. Tomatoes simply had not arrived in this part of the world yet. Nor had pasta! To imagine Italy without tomatoes and pasta is very difficult. But yes, lots of dormice, flamingo tongues, and other critters that might give us pause were often on the plate of a Roman household. And everyone, even children, drank wine, although it was usually watered down.

In Pompeii, so many clues were left behind that in a sense my task was an easy one. After the eruption of Mount Vesuvius in A.D. 79, Pompeii and the neighboring smaller town of Herculaneum were buried and forgotten. Around 1594, workmen digging a tunnel uncovered some stones from Pompeii, but no one realized what they were. It was not until 1709 that serious excavations began in Herculaneum. The area around Pompeii was not excavated until 1748, and the site was not definitely known to be Pompeii until 1763.

The best eyewitness documents recording its destruction are the writings of Pliny the Younger, the nephew of Pliny the Elder, who was then the admiral of the Roman fleet stationed at Misenium. The eruption, which began around midday, was visible from Misenium, across the bay from Pompeii. A man of insatiable curiosity, Pliny the Elder wanted a closer look and also hoped to rescue some of Pompeii's inhabitants. Because the eruption took place over a period of twenty-five hours, he had ample time to sail there with the favorable breezes that were blowing. He could not reach Pompeii itself, but he arrived at nearby Stabiae in the late afternoon to witness the ongoing eruption from the terrace of a friend's villa. Much later that night, he died, perhaps from a flow of the poisonous gases that the volcano emitted.

His nephew, Pliny the Younger, did not accompany him to Stabiae but continued to observe the eruption from Misenium. He later wrote two crucial letters recording what he and his uncle had seen from this vantage point, in addition to the news he later gathered of his uncle's voyage to Pompeii and the final hours of his life, and of his own struggle for survival with his mother. These two letters, written almost two thousand years ago, form the backbone of the historical and scientific research of the eruption of Mount Vesuvius and the destruction of Pompeii. Although it seems unbelievable, it is crucial to note that the people of Pompeii had no idea that they were living in the shadow of a volcano. In their history it had never been active. They had never even suspected that harbored deep beneath the gentle slopes of Mount Vesuvius on which they had planted vineyards was a smoldering cauldron of magma.

There were, of course, many gaps in Pliny's account, which did not begin to be filled in until the excavations started in 1709. Then, in 1863, a wealth of information was uncovered when Giuseppi Fiorelli, a professor of archeology, took over the excavations. Fiorelli is most famous for his discovery of a system enabling him to make plaster casts of the dead. His method preserved the entire shape of the body, not just the skeleton. The mixture of ash, pumice, and mud left after the eruption hardened and sealed the bodies in, encasing the dead in "coffins" of a sort that fitted perfectly. Over time the flesh and the clothing disintegrated, leaving only impressions. The positions of people and animals, their expressions, the most intimate details of their lives were perfectly preserved at the moment of their deaths. Fiorelli devised a way to make castings of these impressions of life caught in the moment of death by pumping plaster into the cavity left by the body.

Of all the research I did and the things I saw on my visit to Pompeii, the most arresting images were those casts of life trapped in that moment of dying—a dog writhing in panic on his chain, his eyes rolled back in fear, or an older man seeming to sleep in a peaceful repose with the trace of a smile which I interpreted as resignation to death. These nameless people, the ones whose casts I saw, who were caught fleeing the gates of the city, falling and gasping for air, became the raw materials for my story. For example, there really was a lady found in the gladiators' barracks, her skeleton bejeweled with the heavy necklaces of a wealthy woman. I was inspired by her to create the character Livia Octavia.

My research covered an array of subjects from the cookery of that time to which fruits and flowers grew or were imported for cultivation in Pompeii in the year A.D. 79. Perhaps the most valuable material for my purposes and especially for the chapters covering the eruption was the work of scientists done in the last ten years. Geologists, chemical geologists, and vulcanologists have now established a very precise timeline, almost hour by hour, of the eruptive events that took place between August 24 and August 27, A.D. 79. This timeline not only documented the meter-by-meter buildup of ash and pumice but the first flow of gases that asphyxiated the people as they fled. I decided to put Julia and Sura well out of the range of these poisonous gases when they swept down upon the citizens of Pompeii in a super-heated cloud. For this reason, it is believable that these two girls would have survived.

For a writer, visiting Pompeii was an almost intoxicating experience. Through this strange alchemy of ash and mud and rock, history had been frozen in time, an intimate history. It was the mingling of the macabre with ordinary domesticity, of the beauty of life with the hideousness of violent death, that I found so compelling. As I walked the streets of Pompeii more than a thousand years after the eruption, I felt that stories—whispered histories of lives cut off, of desires unfulfilled, of love and ambition—were pressing in upon me as insidiously as those ashes that searched their way into every crevice and cranny. Lives were waiting to be reanimated. That is the job of an archeologist. But where the archeologist leaves off, the storyteller's task begins.

Historical Note

CURSE OF VENUS

We know very little for sure about the ancient Roman attitude to physical handicaps. Physical beauty and wholeness were considered a sign of the favor of the gods, from which it follows that deformity could be seen as a sign of divine disfavor or even a punishment for the parents' sins. I have taken some license in making Julia's birth defect a perceived sign of Venus's disfavor, although it's a reasonable assumption, since Venus was a symbol of physical perfection.

Some defects, specifically blindness, seem to have been associated with heightened or mystical powers. Wealthy and powerful Romans often kept deformed or very ugly people as part of their household, and seem to have sometimes looked on them as a kind of good-luck charm touched by supernatural power, as well as a source of amusement.

ROMAN NAMES

The names of Roman citizens usually consisted of three parts: the praenomen (given name, which not everyone had), nomen gentile (family name), and cognomen, which was chosen by the family. Women's names were the feminine form of their father's nomen gentile, which meant that sisters had the same name. In the case of Julia Petreia's family, since her father's nomen gentile was Cornelia, Julia and her two sisters would actually all have been named Cornelia: Cornelia Prima, Cornelia Secunda, and Cornelia Tertia. They would have had nicknames or pet names to differentiate between them. I took a creative liberty by giving Julia and her sisters Flavia and Cornelia three different names, to prevent confusion.

As long as a girl was unmarried, the second part of her name would be formed from her father's cognomen. That's why Julia is Julia Petreia—Petreia is the feminine form of Petreius. After marriage, she might change to a form of her husband's cognomen. That is why Julia's mother is Herminia Petreia.

SIBYL OF SARNUS

The sibyls, who were ancient and legendary figures by the time of this story, were visionary female prophets inspired by the gods. Their origins are lost in prehistory. Originally there may have been only one sibyl, but during Greek times, their number grew until there were nine, to which the Romans added a tenth. Each sibyl was located with a specific place from which she prophesied. The Sibyl of Sarnus is a fictional creation, based on the pattern of the historical sibyls.

STREET NAMES

The standard names usually used for the streets of Pompeii are modern creations, which is why they are in Italian, not Latin. We don't know what the Pompeiians actually called the streets.

FEB 2 9 2008
SOUTH LAKE TAHOE

OCT 1 9 2010 mN